THE MYSTERY OF RUBY'S MISTLETOE

RUBY DOVE MYSTERIES BOOK 5

ROSE DONOVAN

MOON SNAIL PRESS

Cast of Characters at Marsden Court

Ruby Dove – Student of chemistry at Oxford, fashion designer and amateur spy-sleuth. Looking forward to a quiet Christmas.

Fina Aubrey-Havelock – Student of history at Oxford, assistant seamstress to Ruby and her best friend. Avoiding invitations from certain relatives for Christmas.

Pixley Hayford – A shameless journalist on the hunt for a scoop. Not looking forward to spending Christmas by himself.

Elsie Bramble – Cook at Marsden Court.

Alice Ditton – New maid at Marsden Court.

Snave – Butler at Marsden Court. A truly patient soul.

Bruno Daniels, Lord Strathclyde – American-born British politician with an interest in films. A man of oversized appetites.

Harlan Fotheringham – Fina's sweet uncle, who lost his marbles years ago. Or did he?

Penelope Pritchard – Dear friend of Lady Shillington. A herbalist with impeccable fashion sense.

Millicent Sitwell-Slade, Lady Shillington – Fina's aunt and a force of nature. In all senses of the word.

Gerald Standish – School friend and former business partner of Fina's father, the late Hugh Aubrey-Havelock. Napoleonic character.

Marjorie Standish – Glamorous young wife of Gerald.

Clive Studmarsh – Fina's cousin. A rakishly handsome sculptor.

Cecily & Celestia Swift – Twin dancers seeking parts in films. Bright young things.

Basil Thynne, Earl of Chiverton – Friend of Fina's late father. Runs a school for boys. Runs his family with the same discipline.

Felicity Thynne, Countess of Chiverton – Wife to Basil Thynne, mother to young Beryl. Prudish and prim.

Beryl ('Noodle') Thynne – Daughter of Basil and Felicity.

Panther – Marsden Court's newest resident. Fina's favourite.

1

Fina doubled over, gasping for air. The cold ice grated against her fingers.

"I'm sorry. Did I hurt you? I thought the snowball was soft," giggled a girl Fina knew only as Ethel. She was a tall, stocky young woman who apparently didn't know her own strength.

"I'll be fine," groaned Fina. "I think." She brushed the snow from her coat. It was too late. Her coat was sopping wet. Fina looked up and blinked through her fringe. She blew a little puff of air upwards to move it away. Time for a trim.

Amidst the shrieks of laughter from the other girls tossing snow across their Oxford quad, Fina spied a man in uniform striding through the archway leading to their beloved Quenby College. A police uniform. The girls continued to leap about and slide in the snow. He marched through the crossfire as if his constable's uniform were snowball-proof. After treading a straight line through the quad, he suddenly turned left.

Toward Fina.

In her many past encounters with the law, Fina had noticed how a constable's helmet had the unfortunate effect of squishing the face together so the resulting expression conveyed little except permanent indigestion. This constable was no different. Despite the sun sparkling on the snow on this beautiful December day, Fina was already frozen in place by a familiar rush of adrenaline. Perhaps the constable was just walking toward one of the side doors of the residence?

But Fina's intuition – or whatever one might call it – told her the constable was coming to speak to her. She sensed it in the way he studiously avoided her gaze as he approached.

He walked right past her.

And then spun round on his heel. Was this some new police technique?

"Miss Fina Aubrey-Havelock?" he asked, touching the brim of his helmet.

"Yes, I am she," she replied, still rooted to the spot. Only her arms moved, or rather flailed. It was as if her limbs didn't belong to her.

"Good. The scout pointed you out."

"Yes," she said with an impatient exhalation of air. "What is it I can do for you, Constable?"

"Well, miss. I'm looking for a Miss Ruby Dove. I was told you would be able to locate her."

"Ah, Miss Ruby Dove?" It was all Fina could muster while she bought herself breathing room.

"Yes, miss. You are her best friend, aren't you now? We've been trying to locate her."

"May I ask why?"

The constable shifted his weight from side to side and then ran his forefinger through the chinstrap of his helmet. "We're looking to speak to her in connection with some ... activities, you might say."

Although her knees had turned into marmalade, Fina stood

tall. Well, as tall as a short person could stand. "Yes, I know Miss Dove, but I'm afraid I haven't a clue where she is at the moment."

"When might she return to college?"

Fina gulped involuntarily and hoped it wouldn't be noticed. Of course it wouldn't. Not with the high collar of her favourite new coat, which she had purchased on her adventure with Ruby in Italy. "Miss Dove has relations in the Caribbean. She had plans to travel there with her family in London for Christmas."

"Really," said the constable in a low voice. She could almost see the words form through the water vapour that swirled from his lips in the crisp air. "That's peculiar. We know the Dove family sailed from Southampton a few days ago, but there was no passenger named Ruby Dove aboard."

"I regret I cannot be of assistance. Perhaps she decided to travel later and is somewhere in London," said Fina, with an increasing air of social superiority. She couldn't help it. It was her defence mechanism whenever she dealt with the police. Occasions when her double-barrelled name proved rather useful.

"Yes, well..." The constable trailed off and twisted his lips to one side, indicating he judged this to be a dodgy explanation. Bobbing forward on his toes, he scribbled in a small notebook. "If you hear from her, please ring us," he said, handing Fina the scrap of paper with a phone number and *'Police Constable Oates'* scrawled next to it.

Fina stuffed the paper in her pocket, nodded, and mumbled, "I will endeavour to do my best, sir."

And she always did. It wasn't a lie. Just an omission.

PC Oates lumbered off toward the gatehouse under the archway. Shivering, Fina stood rooted to the spot. She wanted to be certain he was heading toward the porter's lodge. After a knock on the door, he disappeared inside. Sighing with relief, she made her way to her residence building.

As Fina stamped her feet outside the door, caked snow on her sensible shoes splattered onto the stone pavement. She rubbed her hands together and blew on them as she bundled herself in.

Inside the warmth of the hall, her brain began to thaw. Constable Oates might be on his way to Ruby's room. The back stairs were a shortcut. There was a risk he might see her arrive, but it was a risk she had to take.

Taking the back stairs two at a time warmed up her frozen limbs. Soon, she was practically flying upward, toward the fourth floor. On the second-floor landing, her progress was halted by a scout.

"Where are you hurrying off to, as quick as a March wind?" Mabel leaned against her broom.

"I must rush to Ruby's room. Now. Please let me past."

Mabel blocked the staircase as if she were a royal palace sentry, armed with a rifle rather than a broom. "I know you, Miss Aubrey-Havelock. You're a troublemaker. I remember everything that happened here a few months ago. The other scouts told me to keep an eye on you. And here you are, tearing up the stairs for no good reason. I have a mind to report you to the head scout, I do."

Fina's small hand balled into a fist. "Mabel. This is urgent and personal. I will report *you* to the head scout if you do not let me pass."

Mabel's eyes floated this way and that as if they were rolling around freely, like marbles in her eye sockets.

"If you let me go, I won't tell the head scout about whatever it is you get up to at night. That is not part of college rules," Fina said mysteriously. She had no idea if Mabel did anything at night – she probably said her prayers and went to bed early – but it was worth a go.

Mabel's earlobes turned a dusty shade of pink. "Well. Just you mind you don't get in trouble. Hear me?" She stepped aside and moved the broom in an overly dramatic sweeping motion. Fina let out a great sigh as she gripped the railing and pulled herself up the next set of stairs. She had lost valuable time, but she might still make it.

On the fourth-floor landing, she poked her head into the corridor.

Silence.

The residents must be slumbering away in their beds. It was a Saturday, after all. Or else they were on the quad, wreaking merry havoc. Ruby's room was the third door to the left of the landing. The one with a mistletoe sprig hanging above it. Fina had teased Ruby about it because hanging it up was such an un-Ruby thing to do. Ruby had said in serious tones that it was a talisman. Not for kissing. Besides, her erstwhile boyfriend, Ian Clavering, was not in college. After their *Train Blanc* adventure, they'd left him in London. And Ruby hadn't heard from him again.

Fina dashed down the corridor and tapped on Ruby's door. A shuffling noise came from somewhere, but she couldn't figure out the source. She tapped again.

Thud. Heavy footsteps. And wheezing. Only one other person was large enough to make that much noise – the snowball-throwing Ethel – but her room was across the quad.

Constable Oates.

If he spied Fina, she'd be... Flashes of terrible past experiences with the police rooted her to the spot. Even her hand remained on the doorknob.

A sneeze shook her back into consciousness. Dashing down the corridor to the landing, she flew down the stairs until she reached the second floor. A glimpse over the railing of the square-spiral staircase told her Mabel had moved her sweeping campaign to the first floor. Still not wanting to risk being seen, Fina popped down the main staircase to her own room. She fished around for a key in her coat pocket and then inserted it in the lock. Nothing happened.

The door was already unlocked.

2

"Ruby!"

Ruby Dove glanced up from her sketchbook and smiled at Fina. "Glad to see you too, Feens, but why all the enthusiasm?" Her pencil flew across her drawing of a chartreuse silk evening gown. Fina knew Ruby was under pressure to complete a set of designs for a client who had requested at least one gown be finished for a New Year's celebration.

Though it was sunny outside, the room still needed a fire. And Ruby had built an enormous one, topped with discarded and crumpled sketches to keep it burning nicely. The steam from the tea kettle was so thick Fina couldn't see through the windows. Ruby sat in her favourite overstuffed chair, curled up with a rug thrown over her shoulders.

Fina paused. It was a frightful shame to disturb such a cosy scene. But she must. She locked the door behind her and, still fully clothed in her outerwear, slid into the chair opposite Ruby.

Ruby bolted upright. "Whatever is the matter? Shall I put on my coat?"

"No." Fina put a finger to her lips. "We ought to stay quiet.

Until we're certain that constable isn't roaming around anymore."

"Constable?" Ruby jumped out of her chair.

Fina waved her hand downward in a calming motion. "I don't believe he'll find us. At least, not at the moment. He's at your door, searching for you. I hope you've stored away any incriminating items. Related to our activities, I mean."

Ruby's eyes grew wider as she paced in front of the cheerful fire. "Start from the beginning, please."

Fina took solace in the fact the fire was unworried by their predicament. She struggled out of her coat. The room had suddenly become stifling. "While I was in the quad, trying to take a stroll in the sun and not be pummelled by snowballs, a constable approached me. He said he wished to question you about some 'activities'."

Ruby held up a hand. "Wait a moment. Does he mean our anti-colonial activities? If so, I keep all of that material so well-hidden no one would recognise it if they happened upon it."

"I'm as blind as a hen in the night. 'Activities' might mean anything from stealing a policeman's helmet to high treason," said Fina, immediately wishing she hadn't mentioned treason.

Ruby turned on her heel so rapidly her skirt nearly caught fire.

"I realise you have a need to pace, but you'd better move a little farther away from the fireplace. You're already in enough trouble. We don't need you to catch fire!" Fina said.

Ruby moved to the opposite side of the room and continued her movement, in a small circle. "Let's assume the constable is searching – or has finished searching – my room. He won't find anything. What will happen next? What did you tell him when he asked you about me?"

"He won't find anything, so he'll leave or will question other students. But none of them know you well enough to say anything. Only Gayatri. And she'd never say anything."

"She's already sailed for India," Ruby interjected.

Fina nodded. "I told the constable your family had set sail for the Caribbean and that you were aboard that ship. He contradicted me – he said you were the one family member not on the passenger manifest."

"And what did you reply?"

"I said perhaps you had other business to attend to in London and that you'd probably join your family soon. I made it clear I knew nothing about your current whereabouts."

Ruby's shoulders sagged a little. "Thanks, Feens. I suppose that buys us a little time. Although what are we buying it for?"

As if in answer, a light tapping noise came at the door.

"One moment," Fina called out in her best casual voice.

Ruby squeezed herself into the alcove next to Fina's bed. Watching her friend move into place, Fina tripped over the rug and stubbed her toe against the large armchair. "Ooof!" she yelped.

"Anything wrong, miss?" the muffled voice asked through the door.

"Yes, er, yes." Fina winced as she limped toward the voice.

It was Durnford. The head scout who resembled a fairy but breathed fire like a dragon. The scout they called by her last name because no one dared ask her Christian name. Durnford was so thin she had to wrap her apron string three times around her waist. Standing attention at the door, she held a tray with a teapot, cup and saucer, a chocolate digestive, and a newspaper.

Fina's eyes lit up at the chocolate digestive, but she managed to avoid the distraction. "Why, thank you. What's the occasion? Why this sudden rush of service?"

"Oh, I – seeing it was the weekend, and getting close to

Christmas and all, I thought it would be nice to offer the young ladies staying in college some tea and biscuits."

Nice offer, my foot. As if Durnford had ever made a purely altruistic gesture in her life. But Fina had to play along. She took the proffered tray but did not move toward the fireplace. If Durnford was allowed an opportunity to enter, she would. Holding the tray, Fina blocked the door. Just like Mabel had in the stairway. The earthy smell of the tea calmed her. Prince of Wales.

"Well, that's kind of you. I am peckish, so this ought to tide me over until the next meal." She grabbed the doorknob and moved it slowly toward Durnford.

Durnford, never one to be at a loss for words, babbled, "Ah, have you seen Miss Dove? Some – ah, a man, ah, was looking for her?"

"Oh, really. A *man* was looking for Miss Dove?" Fina winked.

"Oh, no. A policeman – a constable – was looking for her. Where might she be?" Durnford craned her neck to see past Fina's arms, her eyes straining as she peered around the room.

"You should know where she is, shouldn't you? You're the head scout," said Fina in a disapproving tone. She was quite enjoying having the upper hand over Durnford for once.

"Yes, that's true enough. She said she was sailing with her family to the Caribbean."

"That's precisely what she told me. Goodbye, Durnford." Fina closed the door halfway and then opened it again, remembering her manners. "And thank you for the lovely tea and biscuit. I shall savour them while I read my new mystery novel in front of the fire."

She shut the door, turned the lock and set the tray on a side table. Then she walked back to the door and put her ear against it. Silence.

Ruby poked her head out from the alcove, but Fina waved at her to remain in her position.

Fina flung open the door. Durnford stood over her, as sharp-eyed as a gannet.

"You can go now, Durnford. I'm sure you have other trays you need to deliver." Fina shut the door and strolled over to the fireplace in triumph.

Ruby wiggled out of her hiding place and poured herself a cup of tea. She said nothing, but smiled. They both knew they'd better be silent for a moment or two more.

Fina half-mouthed, half-whispered the words, "How do we find out why they're searching for you?"

Ruby mouthed back, "Call Pixley."

Fina crept down to the senior common room. Fortunately, for once, no one was nattering away on the phone reserved for students. Unfortunately, however, there was little privacy as the phone was near the hallway. At least no one was around.

Lifting the cold, heavy receiver, she said, "Trunk call, please. Stepney 0303."

The voice on the other end said, "Just a moment, please."

Fina peered into the corridor. Silence.

"Hello? This is Pixley Hayford speaking." The voice from the receiver made her jump. It was so quiet. The hush that comes over a building covered in snow.

"Pixley!" Fina exclaimed, smiling. "This is Fina. No need to panic." She paused. "And I'm fine. Ruby's fine. We're in a bit of a pickle right now—"

"You would be," he said with a chuckle.

"Be serious for a moment."

"Right. A serious tone has been established. Half a tick – is this something we ought to discuss over the telephone?"

"What do you mean?"

"You know, police tapping phones and all that."

"I doubt they've tapped the Quenby College line."

Pixley sighed. "Perhaps, but it's better to be cautious."

"Right." She paused as she tried to reframe the question in a vague manner. "Is there any reason certain people – people in power – might be searching for a mutual friend of ours? Maybe for a different reason than usual, or more urgently?"

"Hmmm..."

Footsteps echoed lightly in the hallway. It sounded like someone wandering aimlessly, rather than an irate scout or constable marching about.

"I must dash. Someone's coming toward me."

"Wait. One word. *Newspaper.*"

RUBY STOOD by the window of Fina's room, wringing her gloved hands and smoothing down the skirt of her grey wool travelling outfit. She half squinted as the sun hit the side of her face through the lace curtains.

"What did Pixley say?" she asked as Fina entered the room. Fina shivered from the chill but still enjoyed the smell of the dying fire.

"Didn't have time to say much before Pat interrupted me. Pixley just said 'newspaper'." As she said the words, Fina's eyes alighted on the newspaper Durnford had brought her, alongside the now-empty teapot. "I take it from your travelling outfit that you're leaving?"

Ruby shoved her hands down deeper into her pockets. "*We* are leaving, Feens. Together. Now. We'll sort out this newspaper business on the train."

"What's our destination?" Fina lowered herself into the chair as if she were suffering from shock.

"Didn't you receive an invitation to spend Christmas with your aunt in Tavistock? That's where we'll go."

"But no, I can't," whined Fina. She stamped her foot and immediately regretted the childish gesture. She grabbed a soft woollen scarf from the chair and wrapped it around her head, as if she were about to go out into a snowstorm. Somehow it made her more secure. Or perhaps she was just cold.

"What other option do we have? We can't hide here. The police will likely conclude you know more than you're telling and will return. Besides, these ostensible 'activities' might be something more serious than we could imagine. And what have you got against your aunt, anyway?"

"Nothing." Fina's jaw set stubbornly. "Aunt Millicent is lovely. It's just that – oh, I'll tell you later. But what about Pixley? We were going to spend Christmas in London with him. Even though your safety is more important, I wouldn't feel right about leaving him alone."

"Could you wangle an invitation from your aunt? Didn't you tell me she said you could bring a few guests along?"

"Well ... yes. But wait. Shouldn't I ring her or send a telegram?"

"We don't have a moment to spare. Let's figure that out once we arrive in Tavistock. We can ring Pixley then."

"How much time do I have to pack?" Fina looked mournfully at the disorder of her room.

"Fifteen minutes. I've already looked at the ABC schedule. We need to catch the 12:15 to Tavistock."

Fina would have enjoyed the jolly Christmas atmosphere of the train if it weren't for her higher-than-usual anxiety about what might be next. People laughed, chatted, and drank tea – as well as a few stronger beverages – all around them in the dining car. Boughs of holly decorated each table, adding to the festive feel.

"I may have missed packing a few things," she said to Ruby, who was sipping a cup of tea. "But at least I won't miss my lunch."

Ruby smiled, sighed, and leaned back in her high-backed chair. "Yes. I've learned how cross you become without a meal, even in emergency circumstances."

"I become as prickly as a hedgehog, don't I? You will incur the wrath of the alter-ego of Miss Aubrey-Havelock should you make such a grave mistake," Fina said as she piloted a forkful of potatoes into her mouth. "Of course, hedgehogs are rather adorable."

"Now that you have a bit of food in your stomach, let's do what we do best – besides designing gowns for the rich and famous."

"Yes, Watson," said Fina, removing the folded-up newspaper from her bag.

"Watson?" Ruby cleared her throat.

"Only pulling your leg. I'm happily Dr Watson. Except I don't particularly enjoy blood."

"Nice to have the old Fina return." Ruby smiled. She took the newspaper and read the headlines aloud.

"*December 23rd, 1935*," she said in an official tone. "*Foreign secretary resigns.*"

"About time," mumbled Fina as she chomped on a biscuit.

"*Rowntree's of York produce their first chocolate crisp bars.*"

"Now there's some news I can support," said Fina, picturing lovely chocolate bars stacked high in a sweetshop.

"*Italian children have a three-hour school day due to coal shortage.*"

"Lucky them!"

"*Church of England decides not to admit women to the priesthood.*"

"No comment necessary."

The newspaper made a crinkly noise as Ruby lowered it. "Dear Feens. I won't be able to get through this if you provide commentary – or even a so-called 'no comment' – after every headline. I value your opinion, but..."

Nodding, Fina made a locking motion with her fingers to her lips. She muttered through the corner of her mouth, "Go on."

"*The De La Warr Pavilion at Bexhill-on-Sea opens.*" Ruby frowned. "None of this is useful." She flipped the pages and began again.

Then she leaned forward, wide-eyed.

"What is it?"

"*British scientists reproduce polyethylene for the first time,*" said Ruby, voice rising.

Fina leaned back in her chair. "You would be thrilled, you chemist."

"You make it sound like an epithet," replied Ruby with a little huff. "It's very important research that..." She interrupted herself. "*Police searching for member of Forty Elephants gang.*"

"Go on."

"*After another daring robbery of a West End jewellery shop, police are seeking Lillian Kendall and her accomplice, Ruby Sparks. Both are infamous members of the Forty Elephants gang, a syndicate of women-thieves and shoplifters active in London since 1873.* They must be good – sixty years is a terribly long time to be in existence!"

Fina choked on her tea, spattering the contents over the clean white linen tablecloth. "You think it's a coincidence that your name is Ruby and her name is Ruby?"

Ruby tapped her teeth. "There's a photo of Lillian Kendall, but no photo of Ruby Sparks. That's the third story I've seen this month about the Forty Elephants gang. It seems like their robberies are increasing in frequency. Or at least, they're taking more chances."

"Are they the ones who pose as maids in the homes of the aristocracy?"

Ruby nodded and sipped her tea. "Yes, precisely. I have a grudging admiration for them. On the other hand, I would never want to be caught in such a web of violence."

"So the constable thinks you're Ruby Sparks? There must be hundreds, if not thousands, of Rubys in England."

"It's possible. After all, we're both known to the police. Maybe they're looking for people who keep their first names but adopt different last names. I'm in police files, so maybe they're searching for all the Rubys they already have on file."

"Hmmm..." Fina brushed a few crumbs off the table and onto her pristine, empty plate. "What worries me even more is that it's likely there are reports about you – or both of us – not only with local police, but with the intelligence services. If your name pops up in both places, they'll be even more interested in finding you now." Fina stared out at the blurred white landscape. The day was still bright and blue, but Fina could see little ice crystals in gaps at the base of the train carriage window.

"I see what you mean," said Ruby. Fina turned back to observe her friend. Ruby's hands were underneath the table and Fina pictured them clenched in a ball. "If it weren't for something like this, they wouldn't have any reason to cross-check records between local police and intelligence services."

Fina sighed. "This is another reason we must speak to Pixley. He sometimes covers these stories, even though they're not his favourite. He might have more information. Perhaps he can help us establish that you couldn't have been in a certain place at a certain time."

The smell of orange, cinnamon, and sage wafted toward their table.

"Excuse me," came a soft voice.

Fina and Ruby both glanced up. A blonde woman in her fifties loomed over them. She wore an immaculate burgundy winter coat with a black velvet beret perched at an angle on her head.

"Please forgive my interruption," she continued. "But I couldn't help but notice how you two were dressed in such classic, yet unusual clothes. Do tell me the name of your dressmaker." She was gazing directly at Fina. Though Fina was accustomed to people talking to her first, before speaking to Ruby, it still infuriated her every time it happened.

"Miss Ruby Dove is the one you want to speak to about that," said Fina, motioning toward Ruby. The woman's face flushed slightly, but she complied. Soon, she and Ruby were nattering away as if they were long-lost friends. This gave Fina ample time to inspect the woman. Her clothes and posture indicated that she was either a dancer or had completed finishing school. The latter possibility was the most likely, given the expensive cut of her clothes. Her pursed raspberry lips moved ever so slightly in and out as she listened to Ruby speak, as if the words in her mouth were pushing through to see the light of day.

She turned and walked away, but not before Ruby had offered her a card with her address. Miss Ruby Dove was always on the hunt for the next client.

"A Mrs Penelope Pritchard."

"Glad you can pay attention to more than one thing at once. I'm completely consumed by this problem of Ruby Sparks." Fina paused and stared out the window. "Pritchard..."

"You know someone named Pritchard?"

"Yes ... my father mentioned a Mr Pritchard now and again. Connected to his honey business in some way."

"It's a common enough name. Perhaps it's only a coincidence."

"Perhaps," murmured Fina. "And yet I've got a feeling there's more to Mrs Pritchard than meets the eye."

Ruby smiled as she stirred her tea. "Why don't you tell me why you don't want to visit your aunt for Christmas?"

"Tavistock. Next stop," announced the conductor.

5

As they disembarked into a pool of weak sunlight near the train, Fina realised she would have to explain to her friend why she'd been so reluctant to come on this visit. She took a breath. "My aunt Millicent – Lady Shillington, that is – is the sister of my father."

Though not usually at a loss for words, Ruby only managed, "Oh." She laid a hand on Fina's shoulder as they walked into the station.

The gesture was enough to make the tears well up and Fina's lips quiver. "Auntie, for lack of a better term, 'cut me off' – and my mother, too – after the trial and execution of my brother. She claimed 'bad blood' in the family caused Connor to kill our father. Even though nothing of the sort happened."

"Of course, of course," said Ruby, as they sat down on the benches inside the heated station.

"She never said it, but I know what she meant by 'bad blood', and it wasn't a family quarrel."

"The fact that your mother is Irish and also not from an aristocratic family."

"Precisely," said Fina, stamping her foot in defiance. Though against what, she couldn't fathom. She was particularly defensive about her parents' relationship. "My mother and father met when they were both quite young, living in London. They met in the usual sort of way – through a friend of a friend. When they fell in love and announced they were going to be married, my grandparents – on my father's side in particular – were not happy. In fact, my father's parents were so offended by the match that they threatened to disown him. My aunt took sides with her parents rather than her brother, although they soon let go of most of the hard feelings when Connor and I were born. Children can often heal family rifts. But our family's recent tragedy opened that wound again." Fina sighed and continued. "After time has elapsed, however, I believe my aunt realised the error of her ways, and of her parents' views. She wants a family Christmas – so much so, that's probably why she's condescended to allow me to invite additional guests."

"But you wrote to decline the invitation," said Ruby.

"Well ... I couldn't bring myself to write to her at all. After scratching out a first response, nothing sounded correct. I must have torn up at least ten drafts. My stomach turned to jelly at the thought of ringing her up. I had no idea what I would say. After all, I don't have much of an excuse not to visit her, as my mother is gallivanting on the continent somewhere and it's too expensive to travel to Ireland to see my other family."

Ruby stood up and lifted her blue leather suitcase. "Let's leave this station. It's not as warm as I thought it was when we first walked in. We'll telephone your aunt and Pixley. Is there a place nearby that's on the 'phone?"

"There's a teashop. Bunney's Teashop. Not surprisingly, Mrs Bunney runs it. She's known me since I was a child, so she'll be a friendly face. I'm certain she'll let us use the telephone."

"Perfect."

They stepped tentatively onto the pavement outside the

station. Blessedly, someone had cleared it, so it wasn't covered by ice. Soon, Fina saw the blue-and-red sign outside the teashop. Even though it was still daylight, the glow from inside made Fina hopeful. And sentimental.

The bell rang as they entered the shop, stuffed to the rafters with bric-a-brac. Ruby's head turned with a look of wonder. Children's toys decorated the window ledges and brightly coloured antimacassars were draped over the mismatched, over-stuffed chairs. Someone had set up a cribbage board on one table. Books lined the walls and the smell of bread wafted from behind the counter. The shelf behind the counter was crowded with ceramic bunny figurines, which villagers had given Mrs Bunney over the years.

Fina inhaled and smiled. Despite her mixed emotions about returning home, the smells and colours of the teashop brought back fond childhood memories. Thankfully, no one was in the shop. Must be a slow afternoon.

A stout woman in a green apron popped up from behind a pastry case. "Fina Aubrey-Havelock, as I live and breathe!" she squealed.

Her eyes slid toward Ruby and narrowed.

"Mrs Bunney, it's so good to see you." Fina dropped her suit-case and dashed toward Mrs Bunney. She hoped her warm greeting would thaw any coldness the shopkeeper might display toward Ruby. It appeared to work. Mrs Bunney enveloped Fina in a hug and rocked back and forth.

Then she stepped back and said, "Let me look at you. Appears that Oxford is treating you well. Though I'm sure you're short on scones and proper teacakes. Sit down and I'll bring you a few of the ones that just came out of the oven."

"Oh, no thank you," said Fina. "We're here to visit my aunt, but she doesn't know we've arrived."

"Fina wants it to be a surprise," supplied Ruby. Mrs Bunney ignored her.

"Yes, I want it to be a surprise," reaffirmed Fina. "So may we use your phone?"

Mrs Bunney looked Ruby up and down and then shrugged. "Of course you can, dearie. It's in the back," she said, pointing to a corner of the teashop uncluttered by anything except a table with a telephone.

"Thank you ever so much, Mrs Bunney." Ruby flashed a smile. The shopkeeper's resolve melted a little.

As the pair moved to the corner, Mrs Bunney fetched a cloth and began wiping down the nearby tables, even though they were pristine. So much for privacy. Fina held the receiver and said, "Yes, Marsden Court, please." She took a great breath, enjoying the smell of baking as she waited. "Hello. Oh yes, hello Snave, this is Fina Aubrey-Havelock."

"It is a pleasure to hear your voice, Miss Aubrey-Havelock."

"Thank you ... yours as well," she replied. "Would you see if Auntie is available?"

"One moment, please."

After a minute or two, Fina heard the swishing of skirts and a light step approaching the phone. "Yes. Fina? Where are you, dear?"

"Hello, Auntie. I'm in Tavistock – at Mrs Bunney's teashop. With a friend."

It sounded as if her aunt had dropped the phone receiver but caught it before it tumbled to the floor. "I take it you've accepted my invitation to Christmas?"

"Yes," was all Fina could muster. Taking a deep breath, she continued, "I apologise for the late notice. It's unforgivable. I had prior engagements I couldn't break. Now that those plans have fallen through, I thought I could resume my original plan of spending Christmas with you."

A distinct sniffing noise emanated from the receiver. "It is rather unexpected, but you're early enough that we can make additional arrangements for food and so forth. You say you have a friend with you. Who is it, may I ask?"

"Her name is Miss Ruby Dove. She's also a student at Quenby. We have a dressmaking business together. She is absolutely spiffing and will not cause any trouble. And her family is originally from St Kitts. Isn't that interesting?"

This time a short 'tsk' sound emanated from the receiver. Fina couldn't grasp which part of her response had provoked disapproval. Most likely all of it. Being from the colonies was bad enough but once her aunt saw Ruby was not one of the white British inhabitants of St Kitts, she might be apoplectic. Fortunately, Lady Shillington was one for tradition, politeness, and what was generally termed a stiff upper lip. "That will be fine. I'm so pleased you are able to join us. I'll have Snave send down the car to fetch you immediately."

Fina paused, looking at Ruby as if she could give her permission for what she was about to ask. "And Auntie, there's just one more thing."

"There would be, child, there would be," her aunt said with a sigh.

"We might have one more friend joining us. A man." Then she added, "A journalist." As if that would somehow mitigate the fact he was a man. As if it wouldn't add insult to injury.

Lady Shillington let out a long stream of air, causing a static noise that could be heard by everyone in the cafe. Everyone being Mrs Bunney and Ruby. "Fina, you really do know how to test my patience. What man? And why should I allow a journalist within 300 yards of my home after what they did to destroy our family?"

"I understand. But this man, Pixley Hayford, is a good friend—"

"And what do you mean by 'good friend', Fina? Speak plainly, girl."

"I mean precisely that. He is a good friend. I cannot discuss all the details at the moment, but I can say he saved my life."

"I certainly do not want any further information about that. Why would we trust this man, and why in heaven's name are you inviting him to our Christmas?"

"He is so busy with his job that he'll be alone on Christmas Day."

"What has happened to his people? Have they abandoned him?"

"His family are dispersed among many different places outside of England, so he can't visit them. I'm certain as a cross on a donkey that you will enjoy him. And he's utterly trustworthy."

Sniff. "Well, I suppose I do not have a choice in the matter, do I?" Lady Shillington continued before Fina could reply to this rhetorical question, "I'll prepare for your arrival. You shall stay in the Green Room and your friend in the Blue Room. And your other friend – well, I'll see what we have available."

"Thank you, Auntie, for being so understanding." She rang off.

Fina's shoulders slumped. "Whew. I'm already worn out, simply from speaking to her on the telephone."

"You did well, Feens," said Ruby. "I'll ring up Pixley to give him instructions. If he gets a train soon, he can wait in the station for a driver."

Fina nodded and moved away.

"Here, dear. It looks like you could use a piece of my sponge cake," said Mrs Bunney, offering Fina a thick slice of golden cake held together by a layer of raspberry jam and whipping cream.

"Thank you, Mrs Bunney," said Fina in between forkfuls of

the spongey goodness. "Is there something I can give to Ruby? I'm not sure when our car will arrive."

There was a momentary flicker in Mrs Bunney's eyes but she complied almost immediately. She wrapped a square chocolate caramel in green tissue paper.

"There you go, dearie. So glad you've come home."

"How much for the cake and caramel?" Fina rummaged in her handbag, hoping against hope that a few coins might be lurking in the folds of leather.

"No need. It's on the house. Even your friend's caramel."

With a luxuriant soft growl, a car pulled up outside.

6

Wrapped in the car's warmth, Fina handed over the green tissue packet to Ruby. Her eyes lit up as she bit into the caramel. Then she folded the paper over the remaining chocolate.

"Where does your self-restraint come from?" Fina asked. "I don't know how you do it."

"It's a habit I acquired as a child," Ruby said. "I began to do it to annoy Wendell and the habit took hold."

Fina chuckled. "I can imagine that must have driven your brother mad."

The driver, Horsley, peered at Ruby and Fina in the rear-view mirror as if they were mad as a bag of ferrets. This would normally bother Fina, but it didn't today. There were too many other, more important, things to worry about. Her stomach tightened as she imagined how her aunt would react to Ruby and Pixley.

"We can hardly arrive without a gift for your aunt," said Ruby. "And I don't suppose there's anything we can purchase along the way." The stony face of the driver indicated that he was being paid to take them to Marsden Court and nowhere else.

"You're right. We ought to have something, especially since we're turning up unannounced," Fina agreed.

"Maybe one of us already has something? What does your aunt like?"

Fina squeezed her eyes shut. She remembered that her aunt loved to be in charge. To run everything as efficiently as possible. What could you give someone like that? A calendar? She let the images of past Christmases flow. That was it!

"There is one thing. My aunt is a singularly frugal woman – well, frugal for the wealthy. She loves systems and routines. Her only frivolous conceit is her hatpin collection."

"Hatpins?"

"Yes, and not just any hatpins. Hatpins encrusted with jewels. Hatpins from royalty. Hatpins with history. It's the one subject you can bring up that has her gushing like a schoolgirl."

"That's brilliant, Feens! I have hatpins."

"You? Why would you have hatpins? They're rather unfashionable."

"I, too, am passionate about hatpins. Though I cannot afford jewel-encrusted ones like your aunt."

Fina turned all the way to face Ruby. "Even after all this time together, you still surprise me, Ruby Dove. Do tell."

"I enjoy jumble sales and junk shops. It's a habit. Or a hobby, I suppose, to hunt around for them amidst piles of rubbish. I have a few with me. They're useful for emergency fittings."

"My aunt will love you."

"Well, that might be a touch overstated, but at least we have something in common. That's a relief. And there's one hatpin I found last week that is exquisite. It's hand-painted. I couldn't resist bringing it with me. I believe it will be a valuable addition to her collection."

"Are you sure you want to give it to her?"

Ruby's crooked smile showed there was no need to ask.

Although she had ignored the outside world they were passing through, Fina now peered out at the snow lining the road. Unfortunately, she had selected the wrong time to look out of the window. The road they were on forked into two. One route led to Marsden Court and the other to her old house. The latter was a road that used to fill her with happiness, and now only with dread. The naked, shrivelled trees that lined it seemed smaller than they had before.

"Feens, you look ill. Is there something I can do?" asked Ruby in a hushed voice.

Fina breathed in heavily and then exhaled. "I'll be fine." She hesitated. "But thank you for asking me."

The car continued to amble forward, bumping over every hole in the road. Maybe conversation with the driver would distract her. "Excuse me, Horsley, do you live in Tavistock? Or the village?"

The stony stare thawed in the rear-view mirror. "In the village, miss."

"How long have you lived there?" asked Ruby, playing along.

"A little less than a year. It suits me." There was an edge to his voice that said she'd better not ask more. So much for that distraction. Perhaps his coldness was because his passenger was the sister of a supposed murderer.

The brick edifice of Marsden Court came into view over a gentle rise in the road. The seven-chimneyed, late-Tudor house, built in 1600, was surrounded by extensive gardens, which were now covered in blankets of undisturbed snow. When they were growing up, Fina and Connor had fished in the pond and played games in the walled garden. The secret bee boles in the garden used to startle her when the bees first appeared after a long winter, like drunken sailors finding their sea legs. Although Fina had enjoyed getting dirty and playing in the garden as much as her brother, she did not particularly care for the bees. Honey, however, was another matter. She had never asked her father if the bee boles were the reason he had left his job in London and become a contented beekeeper and honey shop-owner.

On impulse, she leaned forward. "Horsley, would you mind putting us down at the gate? We'll walk up the drive." Anything to put off the moment when they had to cross the threshold.

Horsley's impassive expression was broken by surprise bordering on shock. The thought of anyone choosing to walk somewhere in mid-winter, when they could be comfortably ensconced in a motor-car, clearly astonished him. However, he duly set them down outside the small stone gatehouse that opened on to the long drive leading up to Marsden Court.

Fina breathed deeply as they trudged along the gravel. Though the air was steely, she seemed to smell the clover and hay of those summer afternoons she and Connor had spent here. Her trance was broken only when they rounded the corner, bringing the vast pile of Marsden into view, and Ruby gripped her arm. "The snow ... the house ... Christmas," she whispered to Fina. "You don't think we'll have a Christmas like we did at Pauncefort Hall?"

Fina shuddered. Their fateful visit to Pauncefort had taken place a year ago, after her own family tragedy had been brought to its horrific conclusion. The wounds had still been raw, and the sting of the careless words of that cad at Pauncefort echoed in her memory.

"Aubrey-Havelock... Are you related to Connor Aubrey-Havelock? I remember the headlines," the young man had barked, swishing his scotch-and-soda. "*Irish son murders father, Earl of Tavistock, in a fit of rage.*" Fina hadn't been able to contain her tears. Her grief had marred what would otherwise have been a triumph, for she and Ruby had tracked down a dangerous killer at Pauncefort Hall, as well as rectifying an old injustice.

But she was stronger now. Those feelings were fading and in

their place was a new determination to clear up the terrible stain on her family's name. Connor couldn't be saved – a fact which still broke her heart – but she owed it to him to unravel the truth. The truth about who had really killed her father.

Ruby seemed to read her thoughts. "It must be painful, but let's view this as an opportunity to sleuth on our own about what happened to your father. After all, you have the letter from your brother that you still need to understand."

Fina remembered the letter she had found in the Michaelmas term. Connor had written it only a month before his execution, and it had ended up in an extortionist's box of dirty secrets in a little-used storeroom in Quenby College. With its odd sayings and funny little poem, it had every sign of containing a clue as to what had really happened that day. With a pang, she recalled the curious words in his neat handwriting. "*As our grandfather used to say, I've learned that honey is sweet, but one shouldn't lick it off a briar,*" she murmured.

Ruby nodded, remembering. "I promised you we would solve your family's case so you could have peace of mind about it, one way or another, didn't I?"

"There's no one way or another about it—"

"Forgive me. We ought to be certain as frost that you've tied up every last loose end. Speaking of which, may I ask—" Ruby hesitated. Her consideration for her friend's feelings was clearly at war with her natural detective instinct.

Fina managed a weak smile. "Fire away, dearest. It's easier to talk about it now than it was."

"Tell me what happened, according to what you remember."

"Connor found my father's body in his honey shop at four o'clock. He had been battered to death, supposedly by a stone that was kept as a doorstop in the shop. My mother visited that day, as did a Lord and Lady Chiverton. And someone else, though I cannot remember who it was. There was some dispute over who exactly set foot in the shop. The important point was that my brother had quarrelled with my father over money – that was the motive for the murder put forward by the prosecution."

"And none of the other suspects had motives?"

"It was all rather vague. There may have been disputes, but nothing could be proved. There was an astonishing lack of physical evidence at the trial. I expected more to be made of my father's old friends and business associates."

"Perhaps your aunt might have items in storage that could help us put the pieces of the puzzle into place."

"I suppose so." Fina shivered. "In any case, it's too late to turn back now."

7

A dapper figure emerged from the arched doorway and greeted them. Snave had been the butler at Marsden Court since before Fina had been born. The tall man still had a great thatch of white hair. He shuffled, ever so slightly, as if fearful of falling over. Fina found this rather sad, as he was still a large, well-built man, only in his early sixties. Fondly, she remembered how he had let her run around downstairs and even occasionally played games with her. Perhaps other butlers were like this too, but one only discovered it as a child.

The curtain of quiet outside was drawn back to reveal hurried activity and chattering voices inside. Though the house was decorated sparsely for Christmas, the warmth of the voices and the slight smell of a wood fire were all Fina needed to feel that this might not turn out so badly after all. Her aunt was nowhere to be seen so Snave carried their suitcases, one in each hand, up the large staircase, which was covered in a plush green runner.

An elegant figure floated toward them, resplendent in a belted emerald tunic worn over a long black gown. To Fina's surprise, it was the woman they had encountered on the train.

Snave nodded at her and continued on to their rooms. Penelope Pritchard held up her hand. "Why, it's the girls from the train! Quite a coincidence, isn't it?" She looked Fina and Ruby up and down. "We need to talk about clothes, soon, Miss Dove. I might want to hire you."

She floated away.

"That woman is peculiar," said Fina. "She still hasn't introduced herself to me properly. Wouldn't it be natural to ask me what we're doing here? Do you think she's somehow attached to this other Pritchard I mentioned?"

"It is odd. She told me she was travelling to Tavistock, but that was all. Let's worry about that later. I crave a nice hot bath."

The doors to the aptly named Blue and Green rooms stood open at the end of the corridor. Fina's room, with the forest-green door, opened onto a veritable of conservatory of plants. Ruby's room had a Prussian-blue door that opened onto a calming sea of blue – the curtains, duvet and furniture were all in shades ranging from navy to aquamarine.

Ruby turned to Fina as they stood at their doors. "I haven't thanked you properly, Feens. It appears I've made a pig's breakfast of everything. Thank you for getting me out of a close scrape in college and then finding a hideaway here. You're a good friend."

It might have been the exhaustion, memories, or simple gratitude, but Fina's jaw shook as it always did to warn that a torrent of tears was imminent. "Of course, dear Ruby. You'd have done the same for me."

Stepping into the room before her face became a splotchy wet mess, Fina began to unpack. Not that there was much to unpack, due to her ever-shrinking wardrobe and Snave's efficiency. The large wardrobe in one corner stood open, with three lonely frocks and two gowns. She ran her fingers over the fine-gauge silk stockings her mother had sent her for Christmas. She was afraid to put them on, knowing full well they would survive her escapades for all of about five minutes. Better to save them for summer.

She changed into her bottle-green dressing gown and sat down on the bed. Soon, she found herself lying on the bed, gently drifting away ... until she heard a noise. A slithering noise.

Perhaps Ruby was slipping something underneath her door. She drifted away again.

Thud. Fina opened her eyes and peered over the side of the bed. Her discarded shoe had toppled over, which must have been the source of the noise. But why had it fallen? Her overactive imagination immediately thought it must be a ghost. Her batty uncle, Harlan, loved to scare her with his stories of ghosts wandering Marsden Court. According to family legend, a young woman had drowned herself in the pond and her soul lingered on here. As a child, Fina had considered the pond large enough to be a lake. As she had grown older, however, the story seemed more dubious. It would take a great deal of effort to drown in that pond.

She got to her knees, still on the comfortable bedding, and looked over the brass railing at the end of the bed. A soft snore came from the adjoining door, leading to Ruby's room. She smiled. That must have been the noise. But why had her shoe turned over? It was a heel so maybe it had already been resting at an angle, ready to wobble over.

Just as she was leaning back to lie flat again, she saw a movement in the corner of the room.

A mouse? It had only been a flicker. Perhaps that had been the tip of its tail vanishing behind the terracotta flowerpot.

Or had it been something less corporeal? Fina thought of the drowned woman, and couldn't suppress a shiver. That slithering noise had sounded very like the hiss of wet clothing dragged

363636363636363636363636363636363636363636363636363636363636363636363636363636363636363636363636 across a rug. She fixed her eyes on the flowerpot, willing a tiny mouse-nose to peep out around it and ease her fears. Minutes passed, with her breathing the only sound in the room.

But what did finally edge out from behind the flowerpot was worse. Much worse.

A snake.

8

Fina yelped. She wouldn't have said she had yelled or screamed, but the yelp was loud enough to cause a commotion in Ruby's room. The door rattled. "Feens, are you hurt? Can you let me in?"

"Ah, no, I'm fine. But there's a snake in my room."

The doorknob stopped rattling.

"A snake? Is it poisonous?"

"How should I know? I'm not going to look. And I won't whack up the courage to do so. I'll remain on the bed."

"I'll find someone – maybe Snave – to fetch the snake. Stay put."

But Ruby didn't need to find anyone, because a knock came at the door.

"Miss Aubrey-Havelock. Has something disturbed you? May I be of service?"

"Yes, something has disturbed me, Snave. A blasted snake."

Pause. Fina swore she could hear him licking his lips.

"I see, miss. Am I correct in assuming the snake cannot reach you for the moment?"

"Yes, yes, but I don't know for how long. Can they slither up the side of the wall? Or the bedpost?" She shivered.

Ignoring her question, he replied, "Let me retrieve an item. I shall return forthwith."

"Yes, forthwith will do nicely, Snave. Hastily forthwith would be even better."

But there was no reply. She took solace in the fact that Snave could move quite speedily in an emergency. Like the time her Uncle Harlan nearly set Marsden Court alight with one of his electric inventions.

"Feens, don't worry. I'm sure Snave will take care of it."

"Easy for you to say." She paused. "Sorry. I remember your disapproval of snakes. Not that I'm keen on them either, but I can at least stand them in their natural environment."

The doorknob turned and Snave entered with a poker and a large pair of fire tongs. His face was bunched up in concentration or fear. Perhaps a bit of both.

Fina waved him to the corner where she had seen the snake, as if it might somehow understand her words and be warned if she spoke. Snave glided over to the corner near the washstand. Then, with a sudden movement, as if he were a snake attacking a rabbit himself, he jammed the tongs into the corner. He turned, holding out the tongs in front of him as far as he could, and dashed – or glided, as butlers never really ran or dashed – out of the room.

"Is it over?" came Ruby's muffled voice.

"Yes, you can come in now."

Ruby opened the door, looked both ways, and tiptoed into the room. "How extraordinary. Has anything like this ever happened here before? Is this a common occurrence at Marsden Court?"

A giggling noise came from the open door to the corridor.

Ruby marched into the hallway. "And just who are you? And why are you giggling?"

"I don't have to tell you. You're not my mother," came a small whiny voice.

"Well, of all the blessed nerve. You'd better march right in here and explain yourself to Miss Aubrey-Havelock."

The patter of little feet receded down the corridor.

Ruby returned to Fina's bedside. She had her hands on her hips. "My super-sleuthing skills tell me that a wild snake could not survive the snow – or at least move around quickly enough outside to climb the stairs to your bedroom. I have a feeling the young miscreant I came across in the hallway is responsible. Do you know who she is?"

"Not a clue. If it was a practical joke, however, it makes me feel better. My nerves aren't in the best condition for any other scenario."

Snave stood at the door, hands grasped behind his back. Then he tapped on the doorframe. "Excuse me, Miss Aubrey-Havelock. May I be of any further assistance? I have ascertained that the snake belongs to young Miss Beryl, who also has the unfortunate name of Noodle."

"Noodle?" Ruby and Fina said together in unison.

Snave cleared his throat. "Yes. Apparently the unbecoming title emerged from an accident where the child fell on her head. It involved a stuffed crocodile, I believe."

"Good Lord. That must have been who I met in the hallway. Ghastly manners," said Ruby.

"That must be the aforementioned party, Miss Dove," he replied, the corners of his mouth drooping as he completed his sentence.

"And why is this child joining us for Christmas?" Fina shuddered.

"She is the daughter of the Earl and Countess of Chiverton.

Your aunt invited them. You may remember the earl was an investor in your father's business."

"Yes, of course – Basil Thynne. He invested in my father's honey-making scheme but as far as I recall, he didn't stay the course. Went off to run a boys' school or some such. And Felicity, his wife – I only met her once." Fina wasn't particularly joyful at the thought of meeting her again. Felicity had been slightly scandalised at what she considered to be some frightfully *outré* opinions expressed by Fina. "Anyone else joining us?"

"Well, there is Mrs Pritchard, who I believe you met in the corridor. She is a herbalist."

"She doesn't look like one," said Fina. "I associate them with drapey, shiny, floaty fabric. An ethereal look. Like a fortune-teller, though I suppose that's from the pictures. The woman wears splendid fashionable clothes."

Snave moved his hands from his back to his front, still clasped. His eyes stared straight ahead, as if he were preparing for military inspection. "Yes, miss."

"Out with it, Snave," said Fina. "I'm familiar with that look. I'm family. What's going on here? Don't tell me my aunt, the efficient, brisk, business-like aunt, who goes to church every Sunday – just because it's the done thing to do – has invited a herbalist to Christmas?"

"Well, miss." He cleared his throat. "Since the tragic events of last year..." He stopped himself.

"Please continue. I must know."

"After the tragedy, your aunt fell ill. She didn't wish to concern you. After consulting specialists, one after another, she turned to this... *herbalist*."

Snave said the word as if it were caught in his throat. In his estimation, this profession denoted someone slightly above the rank of pond algae.

"Understandable, I suppose." Fina's voice lowered. "But you don't invite your doctor – or herbalist – to Christmas."

"I believe the two have formed an attachment, miss." Snave coughed.

"You make it sound like a congenital disease," giggled Fina.

Ignoring Fina's commentary, Snave continued. "Mrs Pritchard's husband, a Mr Edward Pritchard, also expired a few years ago. I believe Lady Shillington offered Mrs Pritchard the opportunity to spend Christmas at Marsden. The holiday may be difficult for those who have lost family."

Fina gripped the bedpost a little tighter. "So that's the herbalist, the little brat, and her parents. Who else is joining our ragtag party?"

Snave pursed his lips in obvious disapprobation. "Your aunt has not supplied that precise information. I am aware we are to have nine guests, not including yourself, Miss Dove, or your new friend who will be arriving shortly."

As if on cue, they heard noise coming from the foyer downstairs.

Pixley Hayford's melodic voice lilted upward.

As if she felt the need to explain, Fina said, "Pixley Hayford is a dear friend of ours. Though he is a journalist—"

Snave stiffened at the word.

"—he is a kind and generous person. And usually the life of the party."

Snave pursed his lips still further. Being the life of the party was not the highest praise a human being could receive in Snave's world.

Pixley's bald head bounced up from the staircase, right next to a housemaid. The maid's dark brown fringe had escaped her cap and was now drooping over one eye, giving her a perhaps unintentionally glamorous look. They walked side by side, which Fina found a little odd. Refreshing but unexpected. Snave's frown indicated he had noticed as well.

"It's been donkey's years since I've seen you!" Pixley's stocky figure embraced Ruby and then Fina. His grin was so wide it pushed up his owl-like spectacles further on his nose.

Snave whispered in the maid's ear. Her pinkish eyes bulged as her head bobbed in understanding. From the staccato words coming from Snave's lips it looked as if she had made a grievous faux pas.

Fedora in hand, Pixley turned toward the maid. "I assume you've already met, but this is Alice. Alice Ditton."

Fina shook Alice's hand, hoping it would provoke a reaction from Snave. He let out a long sigh. Ruby followed suit. "A pleasure to meet you, Alice. Have you been here long?"

Alice dropped a curtsy as if she were in some dreadful West End revival. "No, ma'am ... I mean, miss. This is my second week."

The corner of Snave's mouth flinched.

Pixley jutted out his hand in Snave's direction. "You must be Snave. Alice was just telling me all about you."

Snave took Pixley's hand as if he had never engaged in the gesture before, but knew he must satisfy social graces.

"A pleasure, sir. I hope Alice learned to keep that tongue of hers in place."

"Oh, pish," said Fina. "Times are changing. Better to adapt." She spied her aunt trundling down the hallway toward them as fast as autumn days move toward winter.

Snave sniffed. "Yes, miss. There have been changes to adapt to at Marsden Court."

Lady Shillington hurtled toward them, encased in what appeared to be upholstery from a loudly flowered sofa. It was a silvery-black colour, giving her the appearance of a small, furious knight in chain mail.

She launched herself toward Ruby, holding out an outstretched hand. "You must be Miss Dove. What a pleasure to meet you. So glad you could add cheer to our Christmas."

Ruby's face, which had been a study in tension a moment before, loosened and broke into an infectious smile. "The pleasure is all mine, Lady Shillington. You are so generous to agree to let me stay here, especially at such a family-oriented time of year."

"Not at all, not at all!" Lady Shillington's hands flew upwards, toward her face. She turned to Pixley. "And you must be Mr Hayford. I am not keen on journalists, but if you're a friend of Fina's, we're glad to have you."

Fina's mouth gaped open so wide she must have caught at least a hundred flies by now.

Pixley clasped Lady Shillington's hands with both of his own, forming an intimate and grateful gesture.

Lady Shillington spun on her heels and wrapped Fina in a bear hug. "It's so lovely to see you, dearest Red." Lady Shillington took a step back and surveyed her niece. "And you look quite healthy."

Fina tried to shut her jaw, but the hinge seemed to have stuck in place. "Dearest Auntie. Thank you so much for putting up with our rather last-minute request to join you for Christmas—"

"And for including us," said Ruby.

Her aunt's dyed dark brown head nodded. Another peculiarity. Aunt Millicent had always worn her long hair in a bun. Now it was tinted and cut into a fashionable finger wave. "You young people always add energy to Christmas, so I'm delighted you could join us."

"Who else is on the guest list?" A slow drip of dread spread through Fina's body.

"A few of your relatives, Fina. And I believe you've already met, or at least seen, Penelope Pritchard. She's a herbalist. And a few others. You'll meet them soon enough," she chirped.

"Will we meet them at drinks?" asked Ruby.

Lady Shillington let out a little puff of air that was a cross between a giggle and 'psh'. "Well, we will convene during the traditional cocktail hour, but we will not be imbibing alcohol."

"What do you mean, no alcohol?" Fina heard her voice go up an octave. No alcohol to smooth the usual awkward introductions? How could her aunt suddenly transform into the life of the party from a brisk, efficient, no-nonsense woman – but not serve alcohol?

Her aunt's mouth twisted into a lopsided grin. "Do not agitate yourself, sweet Red. There will be plenty of drinks at dinner and throughout the night. We shouldn't be drinking alcohol, however, when we go through a purification process."

9

Ruby, Pixley, and Fina leaned in closer.

"Pardon me." Pixley adjusted his spectacles. "Did you say purification?"

A burst of laughter tumbled forth from Lady Shillington. Her chin shook in much the same way Pixley's did when he was enjoying himself. Her eyes glistened. She put a hand on Pixley's arm and then on Ruby's. "Please forgive me, dears. I couldn't help myself."

Though Alice had vanished, Snave stood still next to them, and Fina swore she detected a slight shaking of his head. He withdrew a handkerchief from his breast pocket and handed it to Lady Shillington.

Lady Shillington dabbed her eyes with the cloth. "Last month, I had builders install a replica of a Turkish *hammam* – or steam bath – next to the winter garden. It was just an empty spot filled with lawn, so I thought we ought to put it to use. I visited several *hammam* when I was in Istanbul this spring."

"Then it's fortunate I brought my swimming costume," said Ruby. Pixley looked at her with a mixture of admiration and slight disdain.

"Well done, Miss Dove, well done," said Lady Shillington. "I'll tell Alice to fetch our extra costumes and distribute them to your rooms. We have plenty for everyone."

"I must say, Aunt Millie, you've certainly brought Marsden Court, er, up to date," said Fina, fighting the impulse to admit she'd liked it as it was.

Lady Shillington chuckled. "It's true, there have been a few changes. Wait until you see the film-screening room! I'm a perfect martyr for Clark Gable."

A clock chimed four times in the distance.

"Splendid. See you all in two hours at the *hammam*!" Lady Shillington toddled off down the corridor, Snave walking at a leisurely pace behind her.

Ruby turned to Fina. "'Red'?" She smiled.

"Yes, yes, Red," said Pixley, who adored nicknames of any kind. "I'll be happy to speculate. Your hair used to be redder when you were a child than it is now."

"Only family call me Red," said Fina. "Of course, you're like family, but I prefer Feens. My hair was redder when I was younger, but the nickname comes from this unfortunate pattern." She pointed at her own neck. The warmth had crept up it as soon as Ruby had mentioned the word 'red'.

Ever the good friend, Ruby changed the subject. "What has come over your aunt? I thought you said she was staid and efficient. With a name like Millicent, it would fit."

Pixley broke in. "I'd love to hear all about your aunt's proclivities, but do you mind if I put my suitcase away?"

"Of course," said Fina. "Let me show you to it. Snave said you'll be in the Purple Room."

"My favourite colour," grinned Pixley.

The trio made their way to the aptly named room. The door was painted a rich royal purple, adorned with a hanging sprig of dried lavender.

Pixley pushed his spectacles up his nose as he opened the door. "Rather garish and daring for an old manor house, isn't it?"

"The generation before my aunt's generation had a rather eccentric uncle who took over Marsden Court for a short while. During that time, he made several renovations. Some of those remain, such as the mirrored blue peacock statues in the winter garden – and our three rooms."

"That's a shame," said Pixley, his back to them as he put his suitcase on the purple duvet on the purple four-poster bed. "It livens up the place. These old stately homes can be terribly stuffy."

"So this brings us back to your aunt." Ruby leaned against the door frame, watching Pixley unpack with the precision of someone who travels a great deal.

"I cannot understand what happened. This is a complete transformation. Do you think she's gone round the bend?"

"I suppose we all have our different ways of dealing with grief. It's possible this is in reaction to what happened to your family. Not that I'm Dr Freud, but it seems plausible. Everything she thought she had been doing to protect herself and her family went astray."

"Perhaps." Fina gave a little halting sigh. "And it's less intimidating to deal with her in this state."

Pixley held out his hands as if he were ready to take a bow. "I've finished. And I'm at your service. Ruby told me everything over the telephone – the Forty Elephants Gang, PC Oates, and your lucky escape here."

Ruby looked at her small silver watch. "We have just enough time for a snoop around."

"Snooping for what?" Pixley shut the door on the screaming purple room.

"We need to solve the mystery of what, exactly, happened to Fina's father." Ruby put a hand on her friend's shoulder.

Fina gulped. "I agree. Let's see what we can find. All of my father's and brother's belongings are here, at Marsden Court. And I have a good idea of where that might be. The cellar."

Ruby groaned. "No more cellars! Not after what happened in Sardinia."

"Don't worry." Fina led the way downstairs, with Pixley and Ruby in tow. "This cellar is similar only in terms of its location. And yes, there's wine, but no wine vats. No grapes. No opportunity for, well, accidents. Or murders."

"Murder?"

The trio spun round. A short man and a tall woman approached from the hallway. The man bore a rather unfortunate resemblance to Napoleon. He even wore his coat on his shoulders as if it were a cape. His round baby face made his age indeterminate, though his thinning and greying hair suggested he was at least in his forties. The impossibly blonde woman next to him, however, looked to be in her early thirties. She had a long oval face with fashionable, barely-there eyebrows above blue sapphire eyes.

"Fina!" He had forgotten to follow up on his utterance of the word 'murder'.

Fina's teeth ran along her bottom lip. Surely she'd seen this man before. She smiled and put out a hand toward him, hoping the gesture might cudgel her memory.

"Don't you remember me? Gerald Standish. Your father's friend from his old school days. And former business partner when he was in the city."

"Oh, yes. I'm terribly sorry. I blocked…"

"Quite understandable, quite understandable." Gerald's chin doubled as his mouth formed a frown. He looked as if he were considering an important, but somewhat dubious, business deal. "Won't you introduce me to your friends?" He gestured toward Pixley and Ruby as if they were pieces of furniture that had wandered into the hallway of their own accord.

"I'm Ruby Dove, and this is Pixley Hayford." Ruby flashed a winning smile at Gerald as she stepped forward to shake his hand. The corners of his mouth lifted and his eyebrows allowed themselves to move back to their customary position.

Pixley stuck out his hand as if he were an American politician ready to close a deal. "Pleased to meet you, Mr Standish. A great pleasure. I've heard about some of your business deals. I'm a journalist."

Gerald's chin redoubled its efforts.

"Please, you may rest easy," Pixley reassured him. "I'm a journalist with ethics. I'm here to enjoy the Yuletide spirit."

"Darling, aren't you going to introduce me?" Her voice was deep and sonorous, as if she might have had a past career in radio.

"Oh, yes. Sorry, darling." Gerald mopped his brow with a handkerchief as if this encounter were a high-pressure negotiation. "This is my wife, Marjorie." He turned to Pixley and Ruby. "After my dear wife died two years ago, I was blessed enough to find this young woman to marry me."

Marjorie handed the book she had underneath her arm to Gerald. Fina had a rudimentary grasp of German, but her interest in politics meant she didn't need to translate the title. *Die Massenpsychologie des Faschismus.* Hmmm. A lesson never to judge a book by its cover. Fina winced inwardly at her own pun.

She looked up to see Marjorie's hand outstretched, as if she ought to kiss it. And indeed, it would have been appropriate, given the size of the topaz ring on her finger.

Before she could react to this perplexing social signal, Marjorie pulled it away and said, "You must have a tenacious spirit, Miss Aubrey-Havelock, to endure the trials and tribulations of your family over the past few years."

Either embarrassed by or oblivious to this comment, Gerald said, "Must dash, all. I ought to ring my secretary. We'll see you all later at dinner, I believe. Toodle-pip and all that."

As Gerald marched and Marjorie toddled away, Ruby leaned over and said, "Toodle-pip?"

"I believe he's trying to relate to us, since we're young. Perhaps he thinks we're bright young things, even though that went out of fashion at least five years ago."

"Did you notice Marjorie's choice of reading material?" Fina shivered.

Ruby nodded. "I did. Something about fascism?"

"Yes. We read about it this term. A famous book about why the masses accept or even encourage dictators."

Pixley shrugged. "I have little time for the likes of the Standishes. Let's get on to the cellar before we encounter anyone else, shall we?"

10

Blinking in the darkness, Fina shook her torch.

"Blast it. The blessed machine won't turn on."

"Let me feel the wall to see if there's a light switch," said Ruby.

Soon, the cellar was bathed in a faint glow that did nothing to counter the deep, damp chill in the air. Off to one side stood a few wine racks. In the other corner stood a shelf with preserves and various jars of pickles. A jar of raspberry jam was calling Fina's name, but she ignored it.

"There's a small room over there." Fina pointed to a door with peeling paint. It looked as if it hadn't been opened in years.

Ruby jiggled the doorknob. She shook her head. Then she pulled out a small embroidered box, opened it and removed a straight pin. "Feens, can you shake your torch again to see if it works? I need a little more light thrown on the subject." She crouched down and fiddled with the pin in the lock.

Pixley took the torch from Fina and gave it a satisfying *thwack* against a nearby crate.

"Well done, well done," said Fina as he shone the torchlight on the keyhole.

Ruby's face twisted and turned. *Click*. She opened the door, only to sneeze so strongly that it swung closed again. Then, in rapid succession, two more sneezes. She pulled out her grandmother's sky-blue handkerchief and covered her mouth. She sighed. And then the sneezing started again. "I'd better step out. There must be something I'm allergic to. It might be the dust."

Fina wrinkled her nose. "Mildew. Or mould. That must be what's causing it. Why don't you wait upstairs while we have a poke around?"

As Ruby left the room, Pixley slid a few crates to the side. Fina spied a photograph of her family on top of one crate and turned away. She began to shake.

Pixley straightened up and said, "You'd best leave the room, too. Leave it to me. Remember, I'm a journalist."

"But how will you know what to look for?"

"Trust me. Ruby's told me enough about your story. And besides, I'm friends with a few chaps who covered your family's story as it was, well, unfolding." He paused. "Or perhaps unravelling is a better way to put it."

Fina hadn't even noticed she was crying until the tears splashed off her chin and onto her hands. Pixley put a hand on her shoulder. "Why don't you and Ruby go upstairs and prepare for the bathhouse? I'll bring up anything of interest."

Powerless to do anything but give a weak nod, Fina fled the cellar.

IN THE LIGHT of Fina's green room, everything seemed normal. As if going above ground had set everything to rights. After washing her face in the washbasin she looked around for the promised swimming costume. It was sitting on her bed in a small folded square.

Ruby came in as Fina unfolded the costume. It was a hessian fabric in a hideous mustard colour. Ruby giggled as she touched it. "Must have been from your aunt's youth."

Indeed it was. In fact, it wasn't a bathing costume of any kind. It was an Edwardian swimming costume. The kind that resembled a sack with a buttoned belt at the waist.

"Yellow must have been daring for her youth," said Ruby. "Perhaps it was an early sign that her personality wasn't as rigid as it seemed to you during your childhood."

"Daring as it might have been, it's atrocious now. I suppose it's rather fitting that I wear yellow in the midst of my depression."

"I have something to show you that will give you the giggles." Ruby held up a finger and disappeared into her own room. She returned with a lumpy item in the shape of a swimming costume.

"Selkies and kelpies. What is that?" Fina ran her fingers along the edge of the suit. It was rough and solid. As if it were wood.

"It's a wooden swimming costume." Somehow, Ruby uttered the words without laughing. "I believe Alice left it in my room in case I needed another suit."

"How extraordinary." Fina still stared at the wooden slats lined in a vertical row, as if the suit were fashioned out of a barrel. She snapped her fingers. "I've got it! It has to be my Uncle Harlan's invention. He's forever making new silly items. Such as a wooden bathing costume."

"I suppose it's not too silly, though. If it floats?" Ruby held it up to herself in an exaggerated pose.

"It puts my yellow monstrosity into perspective. I could be wearing that." Fina slumped down on the bed. "Sorry. I don't have much of the Yuletide spirit."

"Cheer up, Feens. Just this morning the two of us could have been enjoying police hospitality. Now we're here celebrating Christmas with your lovely eccentric aunt in a Turkish bath. I mean, *hammam*."

Fina pursed her lips. "You're right, of course. But why would *I* have gone to jail?"

"Accessory, my dear, as an accessory to all my mischievousness."

Ruby sniffed the air. "What is that smell?"

Fina ran to the door and opened it. She inhaled as if she were testing a lovely perfume. Then she half-laughed, half-exhaled.

"Well?"

"It smells like rubber. It must be coming from my Uncle Harlan's laboratory. At least he isn't making wooden bathing costumes anymore."

Below her, she saw a half-naked man walking through the house, wrapped in a towel.

"Speaking of bathing costumes. Or lack thereof," she murmured to herself. "Come on, Ruby. Let's follow the half-naked men to the bathhouse, shall we?"

11

The trio leapt from one stone paving stone to another, as if they were frogs navigating a maze of lily pads. In between each stone lay a thick mixture of muck and snow. Fortunately, the pathway was lit by a series of enclosed candle-like torch flames.

Steam rose from Pixley's bald head as he wobbled and wavered on one small stone. While she waited for him to brave the next step, Fina took in her surroundings with a mixture of bittersweet sentiment and pleasure. When she and Connor had been children, they'd played hiding games in the winter garden. The gardens' glass dome, invisible in the dark, must be to their left, packed with lush green plants interspersed with splotches of red camellias. Even from outside, she could smell that peculiar odour unique to winter gardens or conservatories – the almost addictively satisfying mixture of moisture and earth.

"Feens, can you move on? I cannot move forward until you do," Ruby said behind her.

Fina leapt to the next stone. *Squish*. Well, she had missed that one. Blessedly, she was wearing a pair of house slippers rather than her beloved shoes, which would not survive another mishap. Ruby had already repaired them for her twice by stitching black satin above the soles.

"Sorry!" said Ruby. "Did I make you do that?"

"No, no. I was in another world, so I wasn't looking where I was going. You know how prone I am to accidents."

"If it makes you feel any better, I've already slipped into the mud twice."

Pixley beamed at them from the patio outside the bath-house, as if he were welcoming newcomers onto his private island. He puffed at his oak pipe, a recent replacement for his cigarette habit. The bathhouse was a small, red-brick, perfectly square building, with white columns. An ocean-blue tiled mosaic framed the doorway, lit by a string of fairy lights. Fina dashed in through the arched door, chilled to the bone.

Inside, new slippers stood in a row so she exchanged them for her muddy ones, threw off her coat, whipped a towel from the rack, and filed into the steam room. The low conversation she heard as they entered trickled to a halt.

"Is that you, Fina?" came her aunt's voice.

It took a moment for her eyes to focus in the new steam-cloud environment. She saw a small figure near her, who must be her aunt.

"Yes, we're here." Fina put her hands out to help guide her to the seat next to her aunt.

"Drat," came Pixley's voice behind her. "I'll return in a moment. I forgot I had on my spectacles."

The steam dissipated. Or maybe her eyes had adjusted.

"The steam runs for ten minutes," said her aunt, as if she could read her mind. "And then it turns off for a few minutes. It's a good time to introduce you to everyone. In the meantime, just soak up all the healthy goodness."

Fina moved her towel upwards. She wasn't so sure about healthy goodness. She felt very naked.

Her aunt waved at two people across from her. Fina leaned forward through the fog. "Cecily and Celestia, may I introduce my niece, Fina, and her friend, Miss Ruby Dove." Lady Shillington looked around. "Where's Mr Hayford?"

"I'm here," said Pixley, in front of the door. He had one towel around his waist and one covering his torso. Fina had never seen him without his glasses. He looked like a different person. Oddly enough, he looked more serious this way.

"Pleased to meet you," he said, waving through the fog as if he were dispensing with an introduction to everyone.

Her aunt leaned over. "Here we have Cecily and Celestia – the twin dancers, you know. You'll have seen them in the West End, I'm sure."

"Of course," whispered Ruby. "I've heard so much about them." She gave Fina a meaningful glance.

"Welcome," squeaked Cecily and Celestia in unison. Fina could make out a pair of redheads sitting across from her. Why did their names sound familiar?

"And above them on the next seat is Fina's cousin, Clive Studmarsh," continued Lady Shillington. "The sculptor."

A man with a chiselled torso wriggled down the tiered seating toward them. His damp brown hair covered his eyes. Now in front of Ruby, he stuck out his hand. "Pleased to meet you, I'm sure," he said in a honey-toned voice.

"Pleased to meet you, Mr Studmarsh," said Ruby, holding out her hand lightly. Clive bent over even further, highlighting his crooked smile.

He grasped Ruby's hand for at least thirty seconds. "The pleasure is all mine, Miss Dove."

Pixley squeezed in next to Ruby with his hand outstretched. "Pixley Hayford."

"And I'm Penelope Pritchard," said a voice from the other side of Pixley. "So pleased to meet you, Mr Hayford."

Ruby and Fina looked at one another. There was no mistaking the intonation of that woman's voice. Well, well, Mr Hayford had an admirer.

"The pleasure is all mine." Pixley must have moved away from the woman because Ruby shuffled closer to Fina. Fina edged closer to her aunt, who was now pinned between her and the wall.

Squeaking and squelching came from somewhere in the corner. A tall man came into view. He was perhaps fifty years old, although everyone's skin looked so fantastic in the steam it was hard to tell. His face was vaguely familiar.

"I'd better get in on all the introductions," he said in a voice that sounded like waves washing over pebbles on a beach. "I'm Bruno Daniels, Lord Strathclyde. But you can call me Bruno." He put his hand out to Fina. "I don't believe we've ever met, Miss Aubrey-Havelock, but I knew your father. Fine fellow, fine fellow. A real tragedy."

Pixley leapt up, causing the towel on his torso to fall to the wet floor. "You're the politician, aren't you? From America?"

Fina smiled at Pixley, grateful for the intervention.

"For my sins," replied Bruno.

Fina could hear the tell-tale signs of an American accent. Slight nasal intonation and a definite pronunciation of 'r's. Though she was more knowledgeable about political history than current events, she was familiar with this jute magnate who had been born in England but had grown up in New York. He was wildly popular. Even though his party, the Liberals, were not. They had suffered a major defeat in the November general election.

"I invited Lord Strathclyde not for his political affiliations but for his love of cinema," Lady Shillington said the words 'political affiliations' as though they were a ghastly disease. "That's also why I invited the twins."

Bruno still stood, hovering over Pixley. "I'm just crazy about the pictures. And your aunt here is, too. We have this idea to make a film with the Swift twins here. We've got the cash, but we're looking for a producer. I have a director in mind, but our last two producers have both pulled out of the project."

Fina couldn't help herself. "We know a producer, Lord Strathclyde."

Bruno sat down opposite them and stared at Fina. Even though his dripping hair partially hid his face, and the steam obscured her vision, she could see his piercing brown eyes boring into her. She looked away. Memories of the Crown advocate looking into her eyes like that made it an involuntary reflex.

When she turned, she saw Ruby looking at her with a peculiar mixture of annoyance and happiness. But that was her general demeanour whenever the subject of her erstwhile boyfriend, Ian Clavering, came up.

Pixley leaned over and winked at Fina. "Yes, we're friends with a theatre producer, though he has dabbled in films. You might recognize his name – Ian Clavering."

Bruno leaned forward and put his palms together in a gesture of disbelief. "You know Ian Clavering? I've seen some of his productions. Fantastic. And I've heard he's easy to work with."

Ruby mumbled something unintelligible under her breath. Though Fina knew poor Ruby was a tortured soul when it came to Ian Clavering, she still enjoyed seeing her friend act out of her perfectly poised character once in a while.

"Ian Clavering!" The twins' heads bobbed in unison. One of them said, "We had a bit part in *Flames of Flowers,* didn't we, C? Remember?"

Really. That was the limit. Twins with names both beginning with C calling each other C?

'C' wriggled in her marble seat. "Oh, yes. I wonder if he'd remember us. He was dreamy."

At the word 'dreamy', Ruby's chin shot up from its position on her chest. The look of venom on her face made Fina's opinion of the twins drop like a stone.

A bell sounded. "Time for dinner," said her aunt as she rose from her seat, nearly losing all of her towels in the process.

Bruno stood up and looked at Pixley. "Wait. If you're friends with this chap Ian, do you think he has plans for Christmas?" A spray of water droplets hit Fina as he turned toward her aunt. "Lady Shillington, I realise it would be a great imposition, but what do you say we invite Mr Clavering for Christmas? We could get this film production rolling if he agrees to be our producer."

"Of course, Lord Strathclyde, of course. I'll tell Snave to telephone him right away, with Mr Hayford's assistance."

12

"You fools!" Ruby hissed as they were the last to make the long, wet procession back to the house. "Are you two daft as a brush? How could you do this to me?"

Pixley put an arm on Ruby's shoulder. "First, I don't know if Ian has plans for Christmas, so it's possible he won't be able to come. Second, why aren't you pleased?"

Ruby's shoulders slumped, even as they leapt through the frigid air to each paving stone. "The man is infuriating. And I hate having him deciding when I see him, rather than the other way round."

"But didn't you see him when we returned to London after our ill-fated train journey from Genoa?" Pixley let out a sigh as they entered the warmth of the house from a back door.

"Yes. But just for tea one afternoon. He said we'd see each other again soon, but then broke off our plans twice. He said he had to visit somewhere on the continent for work."

"That's the nature of whatever it is that he does." Fina rushed up the stairs. She exchanged a knowing glance with Pixley. There was no point in trying to rationalise this situation with Ian. "If I say the man is a bounder or a cad, will that make you feel better?"

Ruby's cap, which covered her hair, quivered as she shook it. "I suppose. Enough already –Pixley's correct. What are the chances Ian won't have plans for Christmas?"

DINNER WAS A GRAND AFFAIR, despite the marked bohemian turn in Fina's aunt's character. All the men, save Clive, wore double-breasted six-button dinner jackets with pointed lapels. Clive wore a white jacket that made him resemble a handsome waiter on a ship. The majority of women wore velvet gowns, although they were all different colours: wine red, navy blue, and emerald green.

The guests chattered away happily. It must have been the steam. Fina's muscles hung loosely and she felt refreshed, though after-dinner coffee would be needed to ensure she didn't nod off during the evening's entertainment. Most likely some ghastly singing. The thought of enduring a night of singing made her cosy bed upstairs – *sans* reptiles, please – even more appealing. And a crackling fire. And perhaps a cup of cocoa. And a hot water bottle on her toes.

The French windows glowed yellow and orange from the slightly swinging chandelier above the long, gleaming dining-room table. Juniper, holly berries and mistletoe decorations were interspersed along the surface.

The only note of discontent was sounded by Lady Shilling-ton, who was clucking as she looked at the carriage clock on the mantel. "Why must Harlan always bury himself in that blessed laboratory for hours on end?" she muttered. "Does the man not realise it's Christmas? Mrs Bramble will be having kittens about the goose!" Finally, she rang for Snave and sent him to fetch the recalcitrant inventor.

At long last, Harlan Fotheringham appeared and they all trooped into the dining room. Fina's aunt sat at one end of the table while her uncle sat at the other. Young Noodle – at least that's who Fina assumed it was – perched perilously on the chair next to him. The child's blonde curls stood up on her head in the manner of the snake the child had set loose in Fina's room. Her large eyes and cupid's-bow mouth gave her an air of permanent innocence. She had been allowed to sit with the adults, for the soup course – and longer, if she behaved. Fina doubted the young miscreant would make it past the first spoonful.

The child stuck her tongue out at Fina. Fina stuck hers out in retaliation.

"Really," said Felicity, the Countess of Chiverton. "Please do not encourage Beryl." She turned and slapped Noodle on the back. A bit extreme, but then again Fina didn't have to live with the child. As the countess bent toward her child to administer the punishment, her enormous strand of pink pearls fell to one side. Mesmerised, Fina stared as the pearls caught the light most marvellously. They must be worth a pretty penny, too.

"We're sorry to have missed you in the *hammam*. I feel jolly refreshed by it."

Felicity sniffed. "Herbalists and naked baths. If you ask me, there's a bit too much frivolity at Marsden Court."

Fina pursed her lips. Perhaps it was better not to deliver the retort that had popped up in her mind. Poor Felicity could scarcely be said to be enjoying herself – her posture was so upright that Fina surmised she must have had a plank of wood inserted in the back of her olive-green crêpe gown. Despite the drab colour, the green added warmth to her face. This was fortunate as her skin was so translucent it appeared as if she had been through an encounter with a vampire before sitting down to dinner. As Noodle swayed to and fro in her seat, Felicity clenched her jaw, all the while maintaining a rather unconvincing whisper of a smile.

Next to her sat her husband, Basil Thynne, Earl of Chiverton. Basil had a rather sour-faced appearance. Sunken eyes, lips puckered like a baked apple, and a jutting chin that accentuated rather than minimised the angular squareness of his long face. The only concession to humanness were his rather unruly eyebrows. Did he comb them upward intentionally? It made him look perpetually alarmed – and they were perpetually alarming to anyone who looked at him. He had an astounding resemblance to Count Dracula. Though Basil was an earl, as the headmaster of a boys' school he had a passion for education. If Noodle's spoiled and recalcitrant behaviour was anything to go by, Fina doubted this boys' school would last for long.

"Did you taste the soup, dear? Absolutely frightful," whispered Felicity to her husband. He leaned over and said, "What's that, dear?"

Felicity sighed and waved her hand dismissively. "Nothing, Basil. Enjoying your dinner?"

"Mmmm ... delicious. Except the soup."

That was quite enough of Basil and Felicity. Fina sat back in her chair and accidentally locked eyes with the immaculately made-up woman across the table. Marjorie, the wife of that windbag, Gerald Standish. She seemed in no hurry to initiate a conversation and Fina found herself scrambling to fill the awkward silence.

"I couldn't help but notice your reading matter earlier," she offered. "Have you a particular interest in the rise of these new totalitarian regimes, Mrs Standish?"

One eyebrow rose but Marjorie didn't look at all perturbed. "I always find, Miss Aubrey-Havelock, that it pays to understand your enemy. Wouldn't you agree?"

Fina was taken aback. Maybe there was more to this svelte young trophy wife than she'd thought.

"Do you follow politics in general? I study political history at Oxford."

Marjorie set down her wine glass and studied Fina. "I adore reading biographies of famous leaders – I'm fascinated by their psychology. Perhaps because my father was a psychologist. I find personalities rather more interesting than politics, don't you?"

"Ah, a bit of both, I suppose. I'm endlessly fascinated by unlearning the history I was taught as a child."

"Such as?"

"The politics of trade – sugar, tea, precious stones. The politics of empire, you might call it. Do you find that interesting?"

Marjorie smiled. "I'm afraid that's all a bit above my head."

Above her head, my foot, thought Fina. This one was cagey.

"Feens, would you please pass the salt?"

Fina scooped up the salt cellar and handed it to Pixley on her left.

Pixley covered his plate with a generous serving of salt crystals. He held up his hand to his mouth as he handed the salt cellar back to Fina. "Ian wasn't in so I've left him a message with your aunt's invitation. By the way, who's the absent-minded cove at the end of the table?"

Fina grinned as she looked at the older man with the feathery, snow-white hair. "That's my uncle, Harlan Fotheringham. Barmy as a crumpet. Unlike my aunt, he's always been batty. I believe the polite term is eccentric." Fina paused. "I suppose that's unkind. He is an inventor of sorts, so he must devote all his grey matter to that."

"Is he your aunt's brother?"

"No. Uncle Harlan isn't a direct relation. He was married to my aunt's sister, Clara. She died before I was born. He's different from the rest of the family, particularly my father. Hugh was a practical sort and always enjoyed being around people. Harlan, however, inhabits a dream world."

As she said this, Harlan selected the salt cellar nearest him. Twirling it around, he gazed at it with the loving fervour of a jeweller examining a precious bauble. He twisted his long moustache between his fingers.

"By the way, I forgot to tell you that my search turned up a few items about your father," said Pixley.

Fina stared at her potatoes.

"But they're not important now," he added. "We can look at them in the morning."

Ruby put a hand on Fina's shoulder. "When should I give your aunt the hatpin? We haven't had a chance to sit down and chat."

"Perhaps when we have whatever evening entertainment is on offer—"

The scraping noise of a chair interrupted her. Penelope Pritchard had popped up like a jack-in-the-box. "How – how can you—" She was on the verge of tears. "It's an outrage! This food – this food is poison!" She proclaimed it as if she were auditioning for a part in Bruno's film.

A deafening clatter of forks hitting plates made the rest of the guests jump.

"What the devil do you mean by this, Mrs – Mrs—" sputtered Harlan from the other end of the table.

"Mrs Pritchard." Marjorie sniffed. Her long, dangling blue earrings swung against her pin curls. Was that a look of approval or disgust?

Snave stood behind Mrs Pritchard but somehow managed not to move a muscle. He must have adjusted to Lady Shillington's theatrical guests.

"This food, these potatoes, contain—" Mrs Pritchard paused. "Animal fat."

Noodle giggled.

Fina had never seen so many eyes roll at once. All except her aunt's. Her eyes had widened. She waved Snave to her side and whispered something in his ear. Snave deftly removed Penelope's plate, as if he were a magician demonstrating his first trick.

"So sorry, dear Penelope. I gave the cook strict instructions to avoid animal products in your meal."

Penelope's only response was to drain one glass of water after another, apparently with the hope it would cleanse her body of the animal fat.

Harlan slammed his fist down on the table. "Well, dash it. I enjoy my animal fat, Millie." He stabbed his fork into a pile of sliced meat and shovelled it into his mouth with an air of defiance.

Lady Shillington said, "Oh do be quiet, Harlan. Eat your meal and hush."

And with that, an undefinable pall fell over the gathering. Even Noodle sat still. And there was that old, familiar, almost electric, tension.

Fina cupped her hand and whispered into Ruby's ear. "Can you feel it?"

"What?"

"Something's going to happen. I don't know what, but there are several people at this table who are not in the Yuletide spirit."

13

The collective mood lifted as they retired to the music room for the evening's entertainment. Bruno put a record on the gramophone, and soon the sounds of George Fornby's *Fanlight Fanny* tinkled across the wood floors. For Fina and Ruby, it brought back memories of their adventures in a London nightclub earlier that year.

Clive Studmarsh sauntered over to the trio, who were ensconced in sofas near the fireplace. He sat on the arm of one sofa next to Pixley, opposite Fina and Ruby. Crossing his legs, he ran his finger absently over the scar near his eyebrow. *Connor,* thought Fina with a pang. One summer, perhaps ten years ago, she and her brother had gone to the seaside with their cousin. Connor, in his easy-going, somewhat devil-may-care, manner, had clambered onto a rock and dived into the sea. His head failed to bob up out of the water. A dark patch spread across the rippling waves. Blood. Clive dived in and dragged Connor to the shore. They'd both ended up with scars that day – Connor from his dive and Clive from his plunge into the sea to rescue his cousin.

Fina wouldn't normally say this about many people, but her

cousin was embarrassing himself. Embarrassing himself by leering at Ruby.

In an exaggerated theatrical manner, Ruby opened her clutch and exclaimed, "I forgot. I was going to give a hatpin to your aunt." She turned to Fina, obviously seeking her approval.

"Yes, yes, I'm sure she'd be delighted."

"What's this? Hatpins? I say, aren't those a little out of date?" Despite the innocuous statement, Clive winced. He reached into his pocket and removed a blue and white tin. Milk of magnesia. After opening the tin and popping a few of the tablets in his mouth, he offered them to the trio as if they were a rare brand of cigarettes.

"Yes. Hatpins are out of date." Ruby rose to her feet. "But your aunt collects them, as do I." Ruby spun on her heel in apparent search for Fina's aunt. Lady Shillington entered the drawing room and propelled herself toward them, as if she were powered by petrol.

"Dear young people, what are you getting up to now?" She said this with the excitement of someone wanting to be invited to a secret club.

Ruby held up a hatpin with a beautiful cerulean blue glass head. It glittered in the firelight, like one of Fina's aunt's own sparkling gem hatpins. Ruby grasped it by the stem and handed it to Lady Shillington as if it were a single rose – minus the thorns, of course. "Lady Shillington, Fina told me you collected hatpins. I also collect them. I suppose it's a hazard of loving fashion. In any case, I'd like to give you one of my favourites."

"Oh, it's lovely, Miss Dove. May I call you Ruby?"

"Of course, please do. I'm glad you like it. I bought it from a lady in St Kitts, who made them from glass she would blow herself. It's not as valuable as any in your collection, I'm sure, but I thought you might appreciate it nonetheless."

"I shall treasure it always." Lady Shillington clasped it to her chest. "And though my collection is filled with gemstones—"

Everyone's heads turned.

"—Nothing can compare to the treasure of a beautiful gift from someone I hope I can call a friend." She paused. "Fina, dear, close your mouth. It's unbecoming in a young lady."

Fina's mouth snapped shut. In that split second, her old aunt had shown her previous personality. It was oddly reassuring somehow to know she was still there underneath her cheery façade.

"Dear Aged A." Clive waved his cigarette about, vaguely gesturing to his aunt. "I hope you have those hatpins under lock and key, especially under the circs."

Lady Shillington blinked. "Circs? Oh, you mean *circumstances*. You young people," she said with a laugh. "What circumstances?"

"I've heard the Elephant Gang is moving westward from London. Perhaps they'll arrive in Tavistock soonish." Clive puffed on his cigarette.

Ruby froze.

Bruno marched over, providing a physical distraction from Ruby, now a statue in the middle of the room. "I'm sure Lady Shillington has taken all necessary precautions." He glanced at Clive.

Fina's uncle tittered from his high-backed chair near the fireplace. He held an empty port glass, which he peered at as if it were his conversational companion. Fina couldn't tell if his tittering was in reaction to Bruno's pronouncement or to something that had occurred in his own world.

"Yes, I'm sure she has taken the necessary precautions. There are a few valuable paintings in the house," said Clive.

Fina eyed one of Clive's statues of a bird on the mantel.

"What about your own art? Are you afraid someone might pinch one of your sculptures?"

Clive treated them to a derisive chuckle. "If only. The publicity might make them worth something."

"You had a grand show a few months ago, didn't you, old boy?" Bruno chomped on his cigar.

"Yes, I spent a packet on the event. It was glorious – we had cases of bubbly, the best music, and delicious bits to nosh on."

"And?" asked Marjorie.

"And. Nothing. Not one purchase," Clive sighed. "But a glorious party, what?" He winked at Marjorie.

Marjorie cleared her throat and moved in such a way that she blocked Gerald from seeing any additional winks from Clive. She toyed with her topaz ring. Gerald put a hand over hers. "Yes, I'm certain Lady Shillington wouldn't invite such important personages to Christmas without an adequate security system. Especially with such lovely sculptures created by Mr Studmarsh."

"Yes, yes, dears," said Lady Shillington as she gave the hatpin to Snave. "After reading all those dreadful accounts in the newspaper about break-ins and thefts of all sorts, I asked Harlan to install an alarm system."

Harlan popped up out of his chair, causing his empty port glass to fall harmlessly on the carpet. "Indeed!" He held up a finger. "It is the best burglar system in the county. We set it at night and no one can get in. Even if they have a key. Well, they can come in, but it will set off the alarm. It's done with a series of electrical wires. You see, you put them in—"

"Yes, dear." Lady Shillington put up a hand. "I'm sure the guests aren't interested in such things. It's time for a grand party!"

Lady Shillington was determined to have a party. And what her aunt wanted, as Fina knew so well, her aunt would receive.

Snave lowered the lights and turned up the volume on the gramophone. Then, from behind a wardrobe, he rolled out what appeared to be a light fixture. A spotlight.

"Selkies and kelpies." Fina turned to Pixley. "Does she want to turn the music room into a den of iniquity?"

"Well, if Alice's costume is anything to go by, I'd say yes." Pixley pointed at the wide arched entrance, where the house-maid was poised, waiting for her cue to come in. In a figure-hugging gold lamé gown, Alice was transformed into what Fina's American cousin would call a 'chanteuse'. In one hand, she held a tray of violently coloured cocktails. Lady Shillington happily waved her in.

Ruby tapped Fina on the shoulder. She turned around to see Clive smiling at her and Ruby. He also had a tray full of lethal-looking cocktails in his hand.

Fina selected a bright orange highball. It looked healthy, she told herself. "Clive, what on earth are you doing playing waiter?"

"At your service, m'lady," he bowed.

Ruby selected a cherry-red cocktail. "Yes, what are you doing, Mr Studmarsh? You ought to enjoy the merriment."

"I'm certainly enjoying the view." He winked and swaggered off toward Uncle Harlan, who was licking his lips in anticipation of the drinks tray.

Ruby leaned over. "Your cousin is a rake. Rather handsome, though."

"Really, Ruby. I thought he wouldn't be your type." Fina paused. "And his behaviour is most peculiar. He's not normally a leering kind of chap. Must be the atmosphere."

"Mmmm..." was Ruby's only reply as she sipped her cocktail, staring at Clive's broad-shouldered back.

The sweet sounds of Duke Ellington's *Cocktails for Two* floated across the room. Cecily and Celestia took to the spotlight Snave had trained against one blank wall of the room. They danced, at first a little stiffly. Must be the peculiarity of the venue. Then, as the music tempo increased, their limbs loosened and their gowns sparkled from the metallic spangles dotted liberally over silver fabric.

The only guests absent from the gathering were the Thynnes: Basil, Felicity, and, blessedly, young Noodle. Marjorie tapped her foot and hummed along to the music. Fina touched her on the shoulder.

Marjorie's earrings swung round before her face appeared. "Yes?"

The alcohol emboldened Fina. "What do you remember about my father's death?"

"You are rather direct, aren't you?"

"My friends certainly say so." Even as she said it, she could sense Ruby and Pixley listening in on the conversation.

Marjorie sighed. "Your father was such a good man. Generous and full of life. I believe I saw him the week before the tragedy."

"You didn't see him the day he died?" Fina couldn't remember through the haze of memory who had actually confirmed they were present that day.

"I did see your brother. He was the spitting image of your father."

In the awkward silence that reigned, Ruby saved Fina by saluting her with her glass. She drained the remainder of her blue drink and began to sway. Fina's memories of her father and brother made it quite easy for her to follow suit, downing the rest of her rather foul-tasting drink in one gulp. Pixley was already on his second.

The concentrated alcohol of the last swig threw Fina off her feet, onto a nearby sofa. Next to Penelope Pritchard. She was embroiled in a fierce conversation with Bruno. "No, no, you cannot portray herbalists like that in a film. We are scientists, even artists, but we have been so maligned in popular culture."

Bruno gave her a sideways grin, clipped another cigar and stuffed it in his mouth. He stared at the woman as if she were a rather fascinating animal he had never seen before.

"What do you think of herbalism, Miss Aubrey-Havelock?" He gestured at Fina with his lighter.

"She finds it most stimulating." Ruby giggled as she sat next to her friend on the arm of the sofa. She still swayed as if she were finding her bearings on a ship.

Fina glared up at her friend, not out of anger but puzzlement.

A new song came on. It was one of her favourites – *Truckin'* by Fats Waller. She jumped to her feet and pulled Pixley onto the floor near the dancing twins. He began his customary Pixley dance – jumping up and down without a care about whether his jumping was in time with the music. Penelope sidled up to Pixley, as if he were prepared to take her in his arms. But he was too immersed in his own world to care.

Soon, Ruby had joined them. And Fina danced with total abandon. Everyone and everything was wonderful. She grinned at all of the lovely people in the room.

And then the room began to spin.

Nothingness spread over her.

14

Fina jolted awake. A stream of light peeked through a gap in the heavy green velvet curtains. The weak light indicated that a thick fog hung over Marsden Court.

She flopped back into bed, hitting her head on the headboard. Wincing and rubbing her head, she sighed. A headache had been throbbing between her ears even before her encounter with the hardwood. What on earth had happened last night? A memory of a lovely party and a feeling of euphoria trundled its way into her consciousness, like a slow-moving train.

The doorknob to the adjoining room jiggled. "Feens, are you awake?"

"I wouldn't call this state consciousness, but please come in anyway."

Ruby padded into the room in a purple dressing gown. She looked herself, except for some dramatic circles under her eyes. She, too, flopped onto Fina's bed.

Fina sat up. Her mouth was as dry as a London newspaper. She picked up the water jug next to her bed and gulped the contents down, directly bypassing the need for a glass.

"What happened last night?" she sputtered after draining the jug.

Ruby groaned. "I haven't a clue. All I remember is that you fell unconscious on the floor. Then Pixley. Next was Marjorie. Then Penelope. After that, it must have been my turn because I remember nothing after that."

"Good Lord. You mean it wasn't just me? Do you think there was something dodgy in our drinks? Or from dinner?"

A light *tap* came at the door.

"Come in." Fina tried to push her mane into place, even though she knew it was a fruitless gesture.

Alice poked her head around the door frame. "Good morning, Miss Aubrey-Havelock and Miss Dove. I brought you breakfast."

"You are a life-saver, Alice. I could murder a slice of toast slathered in salted butter. Do come in."

Alice brought in an enormous silver tray laden with two toast racks, two pots of tea, an assortment of jams and marmalade, and two glasses of orange juice.

Ruby's eyelids crinkled at the corners in delight. "Where did you get that orange juice?"

"Fresh oranges from the winter garden, miss."

The pair pounced on the food as soon as Alice had lain it on the bed. As the maid turned away, Fina mumbled through a bit of toast, "Please stay a moment – if you have the time to spare. What happened last night? Most extraordinary. Did we all fall unconscious?"

Alice's alarmingly clear blue eyes protruded. "I'm afraid so, miss. Dropping like flies, you were!" She bent her head and her soft-spoken mumbles gave way to a roar of excited exclamation. "Not the proper expression, miss. But I'd never seen anything like it!"

Ruby sipped her tea and then cupped her hands around it

for warmth. Fina snuggled down a little further in bed. It was a chilly morning. "Do you remember the order in which we all 'dropped like flies', as you said?"

Ruby gestured to a chair. "Please have a seat."

Alice smiled and settled into the chair with a great sigh. "Well, first there was you, Miss Aubrey-Havelock." She held up all the fingers on her hand and closed one. She continued to close a finger with each name in turn. "Then Mr Hayford, Mrs Standish, Mrs Pritchard, then you, Miss Dove."

"That's what I remember." Ruby scooped a dollop of marmalade out of a jar and smoothed it onto her toast like an expert bricklayer. "Who was after that?"

"I can't be sure. As soon as the five of you had dropped to the floor, Snave and I moved you all. We started with you, Miss Aubrey-Havelock. We brought you to your room."

"Who else was in the house to assist?"

"We roused the cook, Mrs Elsie Bramble, from the kitchen. And Lord Chiverton from his room, since he and his wife, as well as young mistress Beryl – Noodle – had retired early. He came down to help us carry up the guests."

"When did you realise something wasn't really wrong with us?"

"Well, seeing as Lord Chiverton has been a schoolmaster, he's familiar with all different kinds of dodgy, well..." Alice wrapped her apron string around one finger.

"Yes? Go on." Fina leaned forward.

"He knows about drugs and things. The boys at school get up to all sorts of antics, so he's seen these kinds of drugs before. He said they're supposed to be inhaled, I think."

Ruby's eyes widened. "It must have been Benzedrine. Strips of material are soaked in it and then inserted in these contraptions you inhale. Some people remove the strips and eat them. The inhaler is used to treat nasal congestion. It's also used for slimming because it suppresses appetite. As we experienced last night, it can also produce certain types of psychic side-effects. People feel excited, confident, joyful, and can concentrate on the smallest detail."

"Sounds like a wonder drug." Fina enjoyed her appetite immensely as she plucked another slice of bread from the toast rack.

"That's just it." Alice relaxed a little in her chair. "It was the most marvellous party before everyone tumbled to the floor. You were all the happiest people in the world, chattering and laughing. I wanted to call in doctors, but Lord Chiverton said there was no need as someone was clearly having a laugh at our expense."

"Do you have any idea who put the Benzedrine in the drinks? I assume it was in the cocktails." Fina smiled as she drank the life-giving glass of sweet orange juice.

Alice shook her head. "No, miss, I haven't the least idea. It was all rather slapdash as we're terribly short on staff at the moment. It could have been anyone."

All three sat lost in thought for a moment. Whoever had drugged their drinks presumably had more on their mind than simply creating a wildly fun party. There must have been several moments when, with most of the guests incapacitated and all the staff engaged in carrying them to their beds, the house and grounds were deserted. Anyone unaffected by the Benzedrine could have gone wherever they liked, unseen. But to do what?

The silence was broken by a scream slipping in through the open door.

15

A horde of dressing-gowned figures descended upon Basil and Felicity Thynne's room from all sides of the square hallway.

Uncle Harlan wore a dressing gown spotted with milking cows. Felicity, the countess, wore a serious beige flannel affair, while her husband preferred the drabbest brown colour Fina had ever seen. They all pressed into the room, though quite a few guests lingered in the doorway.

Gerald Standish, resplendent in a silver and black silk gown, held up his hands at the doorway, as if he were a policeman directing traffic. "Please, everyone. No one is injured or hurt, but the countess tells me someone has stolen her pearls."

"Stolen? But we had the alarm set last night, early in the evening. Isn't that correct, Snave?" Lady Shillington's head was adorned in a gauzy confection that made her look rather like an adorable pumpkin when she sat down, shaking her head.

"Yes, m'lady. I set the alarm, as you instructed, after the last guest arrived."

"But didn't we come in through the back door after we were in the *hammam*?" asked Ruby.

"Yes, Miss Dove." Snave gave Ruby a little bow as if he were congratulating her on her observation skills. "I temporarily disarmed it as the guests filtered back into the house. It was a matter of entering the code once and then entering it again."

"And the only people who know the code are...?" Pixley wore a scarlet dressing gown with large velvet lapels. He looked like a king, except for the fact he was in bare feet.

Lady Shillington rose. "Snave, Harlan, and I are the only ones, aren't we, Snave?"

"Yes, m'lady. With the exception of Alice Ditton. If you will recall, I had to visit my mother unexpectedly, so I shared the code with Alice."

"Yes, well, Alice has excellent references. If she were a pilferer, though, she wouldn't need to know the alarm code."

"Ah!" Basil held up a forefinger as if he had made a great discovery. He sucked in his cheeks and squinted at Alice through his round wire spectacles. "So she could have been the thief. How long has she been in your employ, Lady Shillington?"

Alice's hands balled into a fist underneath her ridiculous apron.

"Lord Chiverton." Lady Shillington straightened herself up to all four feet, five inches of herself. "Alice Ditton's references are impeccable. If you must know, she came to us a few weeks ago."

"Nevertheless, this famous alarm failed to go off, which I find rather telling," sniffed Felicity. "We ought to search the maid's quarters." She pulled Noodle closer to her, as if Alice might snatch the grievous child away from her. Noodle stuck out her tongue at Alice.

Gerald weaved his way through the crowd, marching through as if he expected the waters to part upon his command. "I believe we ought to call the police."

"Hear, hear," said Bruno Daniels. Clive and the twins exchanged alarmed glances.

Lady Shillington quivered in rising outrage. "I'm sorry, but I must forbid it. We will undertake our own search if necessary. After what my family has been through, we do not need publicity."

Fina put a hand on her aunt's shoulder. She whispered, "Ruby, Pixley and I are quite the sleuthing team. We can find the pearls for you."

Lady Shillington's eyes glistened. She whispered back, "Thank you, m'dear." She stepped forward, waving away Harlan and Clive, who were standing next to her. Clearing her throat, she said, "My niece and her two friends, Miss Dove and Mr Hayford, will endeavour to solve the case. I'm sure you all will cooperate with them and answer their questions in a timely manner."

As her aunt was making her announcement, Pixley leaned over to Fina and whispered, "There's nothing to stop the thief from escaping."

Ruby said in response, "But then we'd realise they were the thief. And none of these people has a hope of going unrecognised if the police were to publicise a photo of them."

The response to Lady Shillington's announcement was deafening.

"Quiet!" Penelope moved forward in her gown of a thousand colours. Her hands had been hidden as she crossed them in her sleeves but they flew out as if she were a dramatic orchestra conductor. "What Millie – ah, Lady Shillington – says is what we must all abide by. I'm sure I'd rather have these three," she said, gesturing toward the trio as if they were a group of small children, "investigate us rather than a group of police."

The crowd appeared mollified by this logic. Fina was delighted that she wouldn't have to face the local police, especially as her last encounters with them had been so tragic.

Ruby strode forward and tightened the silk belt on her

dressing gown. "As we are all gathered here, I have one question I'd like to clear up before we move forward."

She paused and scanned their faces, moving her head from one side of the semi-circle to the other. "Who slipped the drugs into our drinks last night?"

Silence.

Noodle broke the silence. "Mummy, what are drugs?"

"Shush, darling. I'll speak to you about it later," replied Felicity. She swallowed and stroked her neck. Her countenance indicated there wouldn't be any discussion of drugs now or any time.

Clive rubbed the stubble on his chin as a slow, amused smile spread over his face. "So that's why I remember nothing from last night. I thought it was because I was lit up like our Christmas tree after four drinks. And I have a frightful walloping head this morning. Well, well, someone was having a laugh at our expense."

Lady Shillington pressed forward again through the crowd. "Are you saying, Ruby dear, that someone put drugs in our drinks in order to steal the pearls?"

"It's entirely possible. But it's also possible that someone took advantage of the fact we were all incapacitated."

"Smashing party. Absolutely ripping," said Clive, leering again at Ruby.

"Ra-ther." Harlan stamped his foot in approval.

"Quiet!" Penelope stepped in again. Perhaps she had been a grenadier before she switched sides and became a herbalist.

The guests obeyed, but the tension in the air remained electric. Alice wrapped her apron around her finger. Gerald had his hand stuck under the lapel of his dressing gown, increasing his resemblance to Napoleon by the minute. The twins, who had hovered like foxes pacing in a cage, now bumped into one another and seemed to think nothing of it. Only Noodle seemed relaxed, twisting her face into impossible contortions for Fina's benefit.

Ruby scanned the crowd again. "Well, if no one will come forward, we had better have breakfast and let the questioning begin."

"It was me."

Cecily and Celestia stepped forward as they uttered the phrase in unison.

"Which one of you was it?" Pixley adjusted his spectacles as if he couldn't believe his eyes.

Cecily and Celestia pointed at one another in a serio-comic pantomime gesture.

One of them – Fina didn't know which – stepped forward. "I'm Cecily." They must be accustomed to this routine. "We did it. Both of us." Cecily waved the large silken sleeve of her dressing gown about. "I can't remember which one of us had the idea, but we thought the party needed pep. Fizz. And we wanted to please Lady Shillington, who was keen for the party to be a success."

Fina scrutinised the other twin, Celestia, hoping for some clue as to how she differed from her sister. Celestia's hair may have been slightly shorter than her sister's identical hairstyle, but it could have been a trick of the light – or perhaps due to her hair being out of place. "We didn't mean any harm. We use the inhalers all the time for slimming and for being energetic on stage when we're exhausted. They're absolutely spiffing."

Basil glowered at the twins as if, Fina thought, they were the devil's minions. She wasn't too far wrong – a moment later, he burst out with, "Drugs are the work of Satan!"

"Steady on, Pops," replied Clive. He had certainly been watching too many American films.

Pixley snorted in suppressed laughter.

Former grenadier Pritchard cleared her throat. "Enough! It's time for the Swift twins to hand over the pearls so we can conclude this ridiculous charade."

The twins twittered. "No, no – we didn't do *that!*" They both laid their hands over their hearts. Celestia said, "You can search our rooms. We don't have the pearls. Honest."

Ruby did her best to regain control of the floor by stepping forward. She studied her watch. "We will interview you all in approximately three hours' time."

"If you don't mind, I'd like to go into the village for some last-minute Christmas shopping. For Noodle." Felicity Thynne put a hand on her child as if she had requested gruel for Oliver Twist.

"I'm afraid everyone must remain here, Lady Chiverton. But we'd be delighted to purchase a few items for young Noodle while we are in the village," said Ruby.

Such as a few lumps of coal, Fina smiled to herself.

16

Despite the protests of the crowd, the trio somehow convinced Lady Shillington that it was right and proper for them to leave Marsden Court. After bathing, dressing and breakfasting, they reassembled in Pixley's room.

"Why are we going to the village? And why make a fuss about it?" Fina plopped down on a lilac chair in the corner of Pixley's immaculate room.

Holding her skirt, Ruby lowered herself into an overstuffed chair opposite Fina. "Two reasons. First, I want to make the thief nervous. Let them stew."

"So it wasn't the twins." Pixley lay on his bed with his hand propping up his head. His feet, clad in brown brogues, dangled over the edge.

"No. I'm not sure why, exactly, but I don't think they're the thieves. They wouldn't admit to putting Benzedrine in our drinks if they were."

"Perhaps it's a clever double-bluff." Fina slipped off her shoes. *Might as well be comfortable.*

"It's conceivable. But I don't think so." Ruby cleared her

throat. "On to point two. The other reason is to see if there's anyone in the village we need to interview about your family."

Fina hugged herself and nodded. "It's a good time to show us what you found yesterday in the cellar."

Pixley slid to the floor, reached underneath the bed, and pulled out a wooden box. Dusting himself off, he got up and handed an ornately carved container to Fina.

"Do you have the letter from Connor you found a few months ago? The one that made you even more convinced your brother was innocent? Pixley hasn't read it yet." Ruby rose and repositioned herself on a bench near Fina.

The letter was in Fina's handbag. She had formed the habit of carrying it with her everywhere she went. Though she supposed she ought to let go, since it provoked horrid memories whenever she accidentally came across it in her bag, she couldn't manage to do so. Carrying it made her feel as though she had her brother with her.

She had folded the letter at least ten times, forming a hard, nearly indestructible little square. Pixley took it and unfolded it as if it were an exquisite gift.

As he adjusted his spectacles, he began to read aloud.

DEAREST FINA,

DO NOT WORRY. *I know you will anyway, but I hope this letter brings some sort of solace to you – as much as anything might. As our grandfather used to say, I've learned that honey is sweet, but one shouldn't lick it off a briar.*

MAY THOSE WHO LOVE US, love us,

And for those who don't love us,
May God turn their hearts,
And if He doesn't turn their hearts,
May He turn their ankles,
So we will know them by their limping!

I have everything in hand. I've made peace with my fate. And until we meet again, may God hold you in the palm of his hand.

Your ever-loving brother,
Connor

PIXLEY LICKED his lips and folded the paper back into its original square. Behind the glass of the spectacles, his eyes glistened.

Fina gritted her teeth to stop the inevitable tears. It worked, at least for a moment. Ruby did not try to comfort her. She knew all too well that the moment she did, the proverbial floodgates would open.

Pixley handed Fina the letter. "What does it mean? I remember you both saying at some point that there was a clue wrapped up in the letter."

"Yes, it seems likely the briar, the honey, the poem, or the repeated mentions of 'hand' mean something." Ruby rummaged through the box. She pulled out a photograph of a young man in his late teenage years. "I say! Is this Clive Studmarsh?"

Fina took the photo and laughed. "Even though his hair is styled differently, you can see he has that same mischievous grin."

"He certainly has turned that grin onto Ruby," said Pixley as he pulled up a stool. "What would Ian have to say about that?"

Ruby gave him a playful punch in the upper arm and he, in turn, winced as if he had been injured.

Fina knew it was best to ignore Pixley's provocation. "Clive used to spend a great deal of time with us in the winter and summer holidays. He stayed with his mother in a cottage near ours on the beach."

Ruby held up a larger photograph. "This looks like a young Gerald Standish and your father." She handed it over but Fina pushed it away, murmuring, "I can't bear it right now – I'll take your word for it."

"And here's another." Ruby flipped over the photograph. "Taken in 1933. According to the writing on the back, it's Lady Chiverton, Lord Chiverton, Bruno Daniels, Gerald Standish, Marjorie Riber, and Cecily Swifton." Ruby shrugged. "Riber must be Marjorie's maiden name."

"Did you say Swifton?" Fina perked up.

Ruby tapped her teeth. "Yes. Perhaps she shortened it for the stage. Interesting that they all had met before."

"Hullo." Pixley pulled out a folded case, the kind that might hold a diploma of some sort. He wiggled his spectacles and read aloud, "*A certificate of appreciation for the work of Hugh Aubrey-Havelock. A true servant of Her Majesty's Government.*" He closed the flap on the case. "It was presented to him by Lord Strath-clyde – that's Bruno – two years ago."

Mouthing the words aloud, Fina tapped the certificate against her chin. "The certificate might be for his business in London. Or perhaps his honey business?"

"Interesting." Ruby examined it. "Anything else you found?"

"Yes. Two things." He held up another photograph and handed it to Ruby. "This is a photograph of what looks to be the entire Aubrey-Havelock family, including Fina, plus the Earl and Countess of Chiverton."

"Basil Thynne – Lord Chiverton – was my father's business

partner, after he left his city job where he had been partners with Gerald Standish. Basil was the investor in the business and my father was the one who ran it. Though I believe Gerald pitched in here and there." Fina stared at the fireplace to avoid looking at the photographs.

Pixley nodded. "I found an old ledger book from the honey business. There are plenty of entries from Basil to your father. Bank deposits. There are fewer from Gerald. I take it the business collapsed after..."

"The honey business collapsed about a year before my father died. Or I should say Basil decided it wasn't working and therefore my father had to go along with his decision. Basil had this odd turn of heart – he decided he wanted to run a school."

"But if the business collapsed, why was your father still running the honey shop?" Ruby pulled at her opal pinprick earrings.

"My Uncle Harlan was so upset that he stepped in to help my father's business." Fina looked at Pixley and Ruby. Their eyes were wide. "I understand it's hard to believe Uncle Harlan could do much of anything but if you gave him a task, he could focus and complete it in remarkable time. As you've seen from our bathing costume adventure, he is quite the inventor."

Ruby surveyed the carriage clock on the mantel. "We'd better be getting to the village soon. We need to ask questions about all of the guests. There has to be more to them than meets the eye."

"You mean the guests who aren't connected to the family?" Pixley rose and straightened out his blazer.

"Yes, both the family and the guests. Something peculiar is going on. And I rather think it has to do with your aunt, Fina."

"What do you mean?"

"Why did your aunt invite only the people who are most connected to your father's case?"

17

Little puffs of steam wafted out of Pixley's nostrils. "Blast it, blast it, blast it!" He kicked the tyre and then winced in pain.

Ruby bent down to inspect the tyre. "We must have run over a nail." She wound her way around the car like a cat who needs to circle three times before finding a comfortable curled-up position. "Stop a minute – there's another one in this tyre, too. Someone must have put them there deliberately!"

"So what you're saying is that we're stuck." Fina thrust her hands even deeper in her coat pockets and made a little jumping motion to keep warm.

"Yes, thank you for putting it so elegantly." Pixley frowned.

"No need to be cross with me. I wasn't the one who sabotaged our jaunt into the village." Fina leaned down toward the tyre, as if staring at it might magically fix the problem. But she leaned too far and was soon tumbling off the road and into a snow bank.

Silence. Then laughter. Fina laughed uncontrollably as she wriggled and tried to get up. The more she wriggled, the more she fell back into the snow, as if it were quicksand.

"She's delirious." Pixley said this with a straight face and then began to laugh. Soon, Ruby had joined in. She and Pixley grabbed Fina's arms and dragged her out of the snow bank.

As the three of them did their best to brush the snow off Fina, a car approached from the direction of the village.

"Hey!" Pixley waved his arms. The car was moving as rapidly as it could in these treacherous conditions.

It drove past them without stopping.

"How rude." Ruby shrugged her shoulders.

"Ninnyhammer." Fina's shoulders tensed. "Clodpate."

Ruby broke into a smile. "Brushing up on your vocabulary, I see."

"Ah, I suppose this rude behaviour is to be expected." Pixley turned toward the car. "The best thing we can do is walk toward the village. The longer we stay here, the colder we'll get."

Ruby and Fina looked at one another. Their shoes, while the most appropriate ones they had for inclement weather, were not made for a long walk in the snow, besides the fact they were wearing stockings.

The car that had trundled past them ground to a halt, tyres crunching against the snow. The driver's door opened and a figure in a stylish, oversized, double-breasted camel-colour topcoat and brown fedora jumped out.

"Fancy meeting you here."

"Ian!"

Pixley, Ruby and Fina said the name of the theatre producer, secret operative, and erstwhile boyfriend of Ruby Dove all in one.

Fina and Pixley rushed forward. But Ruby, either from stubbornness or shock, stood rooted to the spot. After embracing the pair hurriedly, Ian ran toward Ruby. Fina nodded her approval. Ian Clavering had a lot to explain.

He enveloped Ruby in a hug. She stood there, not responding. But after he whispered something in her ear, she responded. Fina and Pixley clapped and cheered.

Ruby shot them a look of venom, but that look only made them cheer louder.

"So you got my message!" As soon as Ian was disengaged, Pixley clapped him on the back. "So glad you could make it, old man."

"Delighted to be here. I only wish I could stop on for the carols and the plum pudding."

A little sound of disappointment escaped Fina, though Ruby's face was a study in maintaining one's composure. "So you can't stay? What a shame!"

"Afraid not. I'm on my way to an even more remote corner of Devon, where I've promised to liven up the party at the Arbuthnots', and I can't possibly let them down. There's a chance Lord Plunket-Dunbar might get behind my production of *Sarsaparilla Surprise* in the spring. Plus, their cook is something of a legend." He flashed his characteristic smile. "All the same, I couldn't pass up the chance to see you lot, since you're so close by. And very fine you look, too!"

Just then another car approached, fortunately at a very slow pace. Ian waved them all to his car. They gladly made their way into the warmth of his green Austin 10. He had a few rugs in the back so Fina and Pixley immediately spread them over their legs.

The other car moved past them slowly, but not before a woman peered in at them from the passenger seat. She turned away immediately, as if she had been caught peeping into a private bedroom, and muttered something to her companion. Her expression was not friendly.

"Now," said Ian. "I deduce you three were on your way into town when your car broke down."

"Very good, Sherlock." Pixley rubbed his hands together and blew on them.

"Yes, close to the truth." Ruby smoothed her hair. "Except that someone sabotaged our car."

"Mmmm ... sounds about right for the three of you. What have you been up to now? Can't you have a relaxing and enjoyable Christmas for once?"

"We'd like to, Ian, but there have been, ah, some complications—"

"As per usual," put in Pixley. He fumbled with his pipe and tobacco tin.

Ruby looked at her watch. "I have an idea. Ian – Pixley and I will explain all, but I propose we take Fina into the village, if you don't mind dropping her off. She needs to ask questions, and buy a gift for young Noodle."

"Who the devil is 'young Noodle'?" Ian started the engine and shifted into gear.

"Don't worry about that. Listen to Ruby," said Pixley from the back seat.

"Thank you. Our whole car adventure has made me reconsider whether it's a good idea for Pixley and I to accompany Fina into the village. After all, we're not only outsiders, we're..."

"I concur," said Pixley in his most stentorian voice.

Ruby turned around and surveyed Fina. "Do you agree? Especially because now that we have one car, if we all went into the village together, it would be four of us trying to ask questions, which wouldn't be subtle, exactly. And Ian can run us back to Marsden Court, where we can investigate. What do you think?"

Fina pouted. "So you're abandoning me."

Ruby's eyes widened in horror.

"I'm sorry – I was half joking. But can't one of you come with me?"

Pixley coughed. "I agree with Ruby. It's better if you go on your own. Besides, if villagers find out that Ruby is staying at Marsden and her name is Ruby – as in Ruby Sparks – well, then the police will get wind of it and that's the last thing any of us need right now."

"I suppose you're right. But I hate doing this on my own. And what should I be asking about?"

"I think your aunt has done us a tremendous favour by narrowing down the field of suspects. I really do. That means you ought to ask about the guests at Marsden Court – particularly anyone who has an obvious connection to your father."

Pixley turned to Fina. "I agree. If you ask questions about your father, everyone will close up like an oyster. Just give them a soft, prompting question and let them talk." Then his mouth twisted. "Although it will be hard not to take notes."

"You forget, dear Pixley, that I have a secret weapon."

Ruby turned and smiled from the front seat. "Oh yes, she does. Though she may not be able to remember what they said, she will be able to remember what their faces looked like when answering questions. She has a photographic memory."

Ian adjusted the mirror. "You're saying that you're going to leave Fina in the village to investigate her father's murder? And someone has already sabotaged your motor-car?"

Pixley's pipe smoke wafted through the car. "You've hit the proverbial on the head, Mr Clavering."

"I realise it's useless to argue with you lot, but I warn you, one of these days there will be some serious consequences to your snooping and sleuthing. Even though it's Christmas, there's danger around every twist and turn in the road."

18

A merry bell jingled as Fina entered the village general store. The pungent smell of earth from the produce nearby returned her to her childhood. She and her brother used to skip into the store with a little pocket money they had earned from chores. They'd save it up to buy lovely paper bags of sweets. Liquorice allsorts, fruit salads and sherbet fountains. And then long sticks of peppermint rock.

Behind the counter, a line of jars still held the precious sweet cargo. Even though she wasn't hungry for once in her life, the sight of them made her salivate.

Focus, Fina, focus.

"Well I never. Can that be Fina Aubrey-Havelock?" A small round man with a bald round head, clad in a candy-stripe apron, ducked underneath the counter and opened his arms wide to Fina. She had intentionally chosen the general store knowing she would receive a warm welcome.

"Mr Scammel! How good it is to see you."

He enveloped her in a bear hug, although he was so small it was more like a teddy bear hug. Standing back and eyeing her, he nodded approval. "You must be at Marsden Court for Christmas. Glad to see you're back after..."

Rather than letting the silence sit between them, Fina pushed on. "Yes, I am delighted my aunt invited me for Christmas. She has assembled quite the guest list."

"Do tell," he said in a conspiratorial voice.

Even though the shop was empty, Fina whispered, "Well, there's the Standishes, the Countess and Earl of Chiverton, Lord Strathclyde, Clive Studmarsh, and my uncle."

Mr Scammel sucked in air through his teeth, creating a little whistling noise. "Lord Strathclyde, you say? The American?"

"Yes, do you know something about him? I'm seeking out all the juicy gossip I can find."

Mr Scammel's head moved from side to side. "You didn't hear it from me, but there's a rumour. A rumour that, well, he'd been seen in the village with Marjorie Standish, back when, er, your family was together regularly."

"No!" Fina used her best scandalised voice, hoping it would prompt him to continue.

The words tumbled forth now. "Oh yes, those two were thick as thieves. Just like Strathclyde was with your father." He held his hand up to his mouth as if he had made a serious social gaffe.

"My father? Go on."

He cleared his throat. "Strathclyde had some sort of business with your father. I don't remember what it was – somehow connected to politics? They would have a pint at the Hissing Hedgehog, but then..."

"What, did something happen?"

"Well, they had a falling-out. It wasn't as if they had a spat in public, but Strathclyde didn't come around anymore."

"What about the earl and countess?"

The merry bell jingled again.

In marched Mrs Trumper. The hairs on Fina's arm sprang up at full attention. Mrs Trumper was a bulldog – in all senses of that word – as well as the village gossip. Fina had been terrified of her ever since she had scolded her and Connor for eating too many sweets. Connor hadn't cared. He'd stuck out his tongue at her. Mrs Trumper's response had been to clip him around the ear with her handbag.

Fina slid behind Mr Scammel. As if that would provide protection.

"Miss Aubrey-Havelock!" boomed Mrs Trumper. "Why are *you* here?"

Mr Scammel remained in his position as a human shield, even though he quaked like an aspen tree. "Miss Aubrey-Havelock is here to visit her aunt for Christmas. Isn't that splendid?"

Mrs Trumper snorted. Her porkpie hat covered a good deal of her face but Fina could see those teeth. As children, she and Connor had joked that she was the village vampire. Her teeth were pointy and sharp, like the jagged metal of an animal trap. The slow, dangerous grin that came over Mrs Trumper's face only made them appear more menacing.

"Hmph. Harlan Fotheringham was always mad. Clive Studmarsh is a wastrel. Sculptor, indeed – no one's idea of a proper profession! And Lady Shillington is a perfect fool, if you ask me. She used to be a sensible woman. Now she has all sorts of unsuitable people up to Marsden Court. Film people. Like that American posing as a British politician. And those two red-haired twin hussies—"

"Mrs Trumper, please." Beads of sweat trickled down Mr Scammel's forehead.

She held up her hand. "Mr Scammel, please. And that herbs woman. She came down to the village and asked inappropriate questions about the Aubrey-Havelocks. And that cat of a woman – Marjorie Standish. Flaunting herself at every man within fifty yards. Even the staff. Snave is a perfect gentleman and Mrs Bramble is a treasure, but Lady Shillington keeps hiring these maids. Who is the newest one? Alice Ditton? I don't like the looks of her at all. Mrs Bunney told me she thought she tried to steal some hot cross buns last week from the teashop."

Fina wanted to keep the flow of gossip going. "We were just discussing the earl and countess." She expected the wrath of Mrs Trumper to continue.

But Mrs Trumper's shoulders softened. "The earl and countess, as one might expect, are the only ones at Marsden Court worth any salt. Sensible people who don't let their standing in the community entitle them to behave in an abominable fashion."

Although Fina felt she ought to be grateful for this gesture, anger coursed through her veins. One glance at her own handbag was all it took.

Fina flew at Mrs Trumper, nearly hitting her head on a nearby pyramid of Bovril jars. She began to thump Mrs Trumper on the head, exactly in the same way the woman had hit Connor with her own handbag.

"You windbag of vile filth and gossip! A fustilugs who couldn't give a toss about other people's feelings."

Though she could barely see Mrs Trumper's face in her furious lashings against her body, she caught a look of confusion and horror. But Mrs Trumper pulled back her lips to reveal those sharp little teeth.

And then she hit Fina with her own handbag. Soon, they were throwing their handbags at one another as if they were using medieval hurling devices.

"Ladies, please!" Mr Scammel protested but he made no move to intervene between the two infuriated parties.

At last, Fina lost her grip on her handbag and it slipped to the floor. She ducked an oncoming assault from Mrs Trumper's green leather bag.

Just as she was winding up to give Mrs Trumper a sock in the jaw, she stopped and eyed Mrs Trumper's brown stockings. Fina kicked her in the shins with the sharp toe of her shoe.

Mrs Trumper screeched, dropped her bag and grabbed her shin as she hopped around the store, causing tins of tongue and tomato soup displays to topple over.

Seizing this opportunity to flee, Fina scooped up her own handbag and dashed into the street.

Over the hedge nearest the shop, she saw a helmet bobbing up and down.

A policeman's helmet.

19

"Ah, that's much better," Ruby sighed, rubbing her forearms. She stretched out her hands in front of the crackling fire in the drawing room.

"Mrs Bramble's a dab hand at putting together a spiffing early tea." Pixley leaned back in the sofa and munched on a triangular sandwich.

"Those scones were delicious. And that raspberry jam was heavenly." Ruby leaned against the fireplace, peeking into the box of cigarettes on the mantel as if they might hold the missing pearls. "Shame we couldn't talk Mr Clavering into joining us. I wonder how Fina is getting on. It's a pity to leave her alone in the village, but she's much more likely to get on with the local people than we are."

"Yes, I'm sure she's chatting away in some cosy teashop with them all right now. Or buying a present for the young reprobate, Noodle, who clearly ought to be gifted a nice strong rod in her stocking this year. So her parents can show her what discipline means." Pixley rummaged around inside his jacket. He withdrew a crumpled newspaper clipping.

After wiping his fingers on a nearby napkin, he smoothed

out the clipping on his knee. "Since Fina isn't here, this is an opportune moment to share with you what I found in the cellar last night. I didn't mention it earlier because I didn't want to upset Fina."

"Is it about her father's murder?"

Pixley nodded as he sipped his tea. He passed the clipping over to Ruby. She rose, took the clipping, and huddled under a reading lamp in the corner. She read aloud.

Son of Murdered Man Found Guilty: Sentenced to Death

Mr Connor Aubrey-Havelock, son of Mr and Mrs Hugh Aubrey-Havelock, has been found guilty of the murder of his father. Mr Hugh Aubrey-Havelock suffered a fatal blow to the head in his honey shop near Tavistock at five o'clock in the afternoon. The police obtained an eyewitness report of a hooded figure leaving the business at four o'clock, though the witness – anonymous and not present at the trial – admitted difficulty in identifying the person, believed to be a man, as evinced by the gait.

Other visitors to the shop that day included the deceased's wife, Anne; his son, Connor; his erstwhile business partner, Lord Chiverton; Lady Chiverton; and Mr Gerald Standish. The deceased received telephone calls from Lord Strathclyde, and his brother-in-law Mr Harlan Fotheringham.

Local constable PC Johnston testified that he was summoned to the crime scene by Mr Connor Aubrey-Havelock, who discovered the body. The murder weapon was confirmed as a large stone found inside the honey shop.

Under questioning from the prosecution, three witnesses confirmed that Mr Connor Aubrey-Havelock had been present in the vicinity of the shop an hour before the crime was committed. All other parties called to the witness-stand were able to provide alibis.

The Crown prosecution put forward a theory that Mr Connor Aubrey-Havelock's motive was anger about being denied a loan and continuing allowance from his father. Mr George Flatley KC, acting

for the Crown, put it to the jury that the hooded figure seen leaving
the shop was in fact Mr Connor Aubrey-Havelock in disguise, and
that the accused then returned to the honey shop later, without the
cloak, so as to deflect suspicion away from himself.

Though the accused protested this theory, the jury found enough
evidence to convict him of murder. He was subsequently condemned to
death.

Ruby shook her head. "What a dreadful story. You know, Pix,
the more I learn about this case, the more I feel absolutely
driven to clear that poor boy's name. Partly for Fina's sake, of
course, but partly also because the whole affair seems like a
monstrous injustice. I simply can't let it slip through the
cracks."

"I agree," said Pixley sombrely. "But who do you suppose the
real culprit might be?"

"I haven't a clue ... but something isn't quite right. It doesn't
match the story Fina told me earlier."

Before Pixley could offer encouragement, the grandfather
clock in the hallway struck twice.

"That's it! Fina said Connor found the body at four o'clock,
but the newspaper says five o'clock."

"Perhaps Fina misremembered. After all, the newspaper
does say the hooded figure was seen leaving the shop at four
o'clock."

"It's possible, but still an intriguing discrepancy,
nonetheless."

A cough came from the doorway.

"The Countess of Chiverton is here to see you, Miss Dove
and Mr Hayford." Snave waved a hand as if he were producing a
rabbit from a hat. Felicity Thynne, Lady Chiverton, appeared in
the doorway. She nodded at Snave and closed the double doors
as she entered the drawing room.

"Would you like some scandal-water, what?" Pixley pushed

the tray with the teapot and cups nearer to Felicity as she sat next to Ruby on the sofa.

"No, thank you." She gave Pixley a disdainful glance. "I'll be brief. I expect you're speaking to everyone and, well, given my rather nervous nature, I thought it would be a relief to be interviewed now rather than later." She toyed absently with the red-beaded necklace at her throat.

"Of course." Ruby turned to face her. "Please tell us what happened last night."

"As you know, my husband, young Beryl and I retired early. It was our customary time to sleep. After tucking Beryl into bed I was on my way to our room when I heard footsteps behind me. I turned, but no one was there. Assuming it was my imagination, I continued on and entered our bedroom. As soon as I did, however, I heard footsteps outside our door. Though it was unnerving, I didn't think much of it as the house is full of guests. I thought it might have been Snave, or the maid, Alice."

Pixley scribbled in his little leather-bound notebook. Ruby glared at him. He gave her an apologetic shrug and stuffed the pen and notebook back into his pocket.

Felicity bit her lip and continued, absently staring at a small blue figurine of a dancing lady at the centre of an end table. "And my pearls weren't the only item of value stolen last night."

Ruby and Pixley leaned forward.

"That gold lamé gown Alice wore – I saw it after the chaos that ensued after dinner – was mine."

Ruby and Pixley blinked at one another. Ruby smiled. "It was a lovely dress. I assumed Lady Shillington had allowed Alice to wear it, though I wondered where Alice found the funds to purchase it."

Pixley pulled up his trouser legs as if he were preparing to wade into a small pool. "Half a minute – why didn't you say something earlier?"

Felicity swallowed several times as if a slice of apple were lodged in her throat. "My husband isn't aware of the gown. He does not approve of such frivolities. If he were to find out, he would be most upset."

"Because of the money you spent?" Pixley squinted through his glasses as if he couldn't see Felicity.

Felicity shook her head. "Basil would view it as wasteful, but he would object more to the message it would send about, well, my, my..."

"Your womanhood, Lady Chiverton?" Ruby gave her a knowing smile.

Felicity let out a great sigh. "I knew you'd understand."

Pixley jumped up and meandered between the furniture in the room. "Now, Lady Chiverton, as to the figure you saw in the hall—"

The double doors burst open. Alice burst in. "Oh please, Miss Dove, Mr Hayford, please come quickly!"

Ruby and Pixley didn't need to be told twice. They flew through the double doors into the cold air of the hallway.

Lady Shillington and Harlan paced past each other like tigers waiting for lunch at the zoo. Lady Shillington's hands were clasped in front of her, while Harlan's were behind his back.

Harlan stopped his pacing, nearly causing a collision with his sister-in-law. Placing both hands on her shoulders, he said, "Don't worry, Millie. We'll have Fina's young friends go and sort it out."

"Excuse me, Mr Fotheringham, but what do you mean by 'sort it out'?" Ruby took small steps toward them at a measured pace.

"Oh, Miss Dove – Ruby – Fina has got herself into a pickle again. She's down at the station."

Pixley removed his spectacles as if that would help him hear better. "You mean the police station?"

"Did someone say police?" Clive marched into the hallway, trailing bits of clay behind him. He wore a brown smock also covered with the stuff. His hair appeared as if it were turning grey, though it was a result of more pieces of clay caked onto individual strands of hair.

Harlan turned on his heel toward Clive. "Now, I suggest that you, Miss Dove, and Mr Hayford here go into town together to fetch Fina."

"Old Red's got herself in trouble again, has she?" Clive flashed a smile of admiration as he bounced on the balls of his feet. "Let's go bail her out, shall we?"

Pixley raised his eyebrows at Ruby. It looked as though they were saddled with Clive's presence, like it or not.

"What's landed her in jail this time?" Clive slid into the over-coat proffered by Snave.

20

"So old Red took a swing at Mrs Trumper. Well, good for her, I say." Clive turned the wheel of his red Singer out of the drive of Marsden Court.

Ruby sat in the front seat with two rugs on her legs, while Pixley sat in back with three. In the rush to leave Marsden Court, neither had had adequate time to dress properly. Snowflakes brushed against the window, playfully spinning and melting away. As they made their way down the drive toward the village, the windscreen wipers squeaked.

Pixley leaned forward from the back seat. "Who is Mrs Trumper?"

"Ghastly woman. Used to torment us as children. Mr Trumper died in the war and Mrs Trumper was never the same after that. I'd feel sorry for her if she weren't such a bitter, spiteful person. She was particularly mean to Connor when we were children because he wasn't afraid of her – and that made her only more vicious. Once he caught her yelling at a small child for skipping down the road with a lollipop in her mouth. Connor went up and told her to leave the poor child alone. She hit him with her handbag until he escaped and ran away. I suspect Mrs Trumper must have said something to Fina that set her off." He chuckled. "It's funny, you know. The whole Aubrey-Havelock family were – or are – mild as lambs. Fina was the only one with the temper. Probably living with a group of people that calm made her even more combative."

Ruby nodded. Without a glance at Clive, she said, "Fina is convinced her brother was innocent."

Clive's gloved hands gripped the wheel tighter.

"And we're trying to help her come to some peace about it. Can you tell us anything you remember about the case? We didn't want to ask you in front of her."

Clive turned his head toward Pixley. "Are you taking notes?"

Pixley grinned sheepishly. "Professional habit, old boy. Professional habit. You don't mind, do you?"

Clive didn't respond to the question but instead poured forth a torrent of words. "What's peculiar about this gathering – at Marsden Court, I mean – is that Auntie has invited all the players from that drama and tragedy."

"Besides the family, you mean?" Ruby rubbed her hands together against the chill in the car.

"Yes, there's the family, all of whom were here when it happened." Clive paused and swerved to miss a hole in the road. "Then there's Bruno Daniels, who knew my uncle Hugh."

"Seems like a nice chap," said Pixley from the back seat. "And he appears to enjoy Ruby's company."

Clive cleared his throat. "Yes, nice enough, I suppose. Perhaps a little too nice sometimes. I can't quite put my finger on it, but I don't trust him. Perhaps it's because he's a politician. And a politician who has been heavily involved in the Irish question. That's another reason not to trust him. Seems pro-independence, but then, well, votes for anti-independence legislation. But I suppose that's what politicians do." He shifted gears as they made their way down a small hill. The village came into sight.

"Looks like a picture postcard. Maybe we can stop for more tea after we rescue Fina," said Pixley.

Ruby glared at him. "Back to the guests. What about the earl and countess?"

Clive grimaced. "Stuck up so-and-sos, if you ask me. And stingy with it. I tried to sell them a sculpture once – not a bad little piece, in fact. But once they heard the price, they couldn't get away fast enough. Do you know what the earl said as we were leaving this morning? He said his wife's pearls were an extravagance they couldn't afford anyway. Then he said too much jewellery made a woman look like a strumpet."

"Good Lord," said Pixley. "He has a stranglehold – I mean a grip – on his wife."

Clive sighed. "To make matters worse, they made away with a king's ransom after Uncle Hugh's death. He left half the estate to them for that blasted school."

"But I thought they had a falling-out," said Pixley.

"They did, but Uncle Hugh didn't cut him out of the will. Or at least he didn't have time to do so."

Pixley licked his lips and leaned forward. "You don't think he had a motive to kill him, do you?"

"Perhaps. Especially because Connor couldn't possibly have done it."

"Why do you say that? Wasn't he seen by a witness?" Ruby wiped the window with her gloved hand. It was getting steamy inside the car.

"Ostensibly. But that witness only saw a hooded figure. Yes, lots of people said they saw Connor in the vicinity at the time of the crime, but no one actually saw him enter Uncle Hugh's honey shop. And witnesses are easy to pay. Particularly in desperate times like these."

"Surely they'd recant their testimony once they saw Connor headed for the gallows," said Pixley.

"Not necessarily. If the real murderer was extorting money from them or had some way of forcing them to keep quiet, then they'd comply to save themselves."

"What happened that day? Pixley and I have been trying to piece together the story, for Fina's sake."

Clive nodded. "I'll do my best. Several people visited Uncle Hugh on the afternoon of his death. Felicity, Basil, Gerald and Connor. Though at least two other figures were seen going into the shop. They were never identified."

"Who found the body?"

"Connor found his father, poor chap." Though he had both hands on the steering wheel, Clive removed one to trace the scar near his eyebrow. "He found Uncle Hugh behind the counter, dead."

"Was he facing outward or did he have his back to the counter?" Ruby asked.

"Good question. He had his back to the counter. The murder weapon was apparently a heavy stone used as a doorstop, usually hidden behind the door."

"So, these two facts point to the fact he probably knew and felt comfortable with the killer – since he had his back to them – and also that the killer had been to the shop before." Pixley's voice vibrated as they hit a rough patch of road.

"Precisely." Clive gripped the wheel.

Ruby wasn't about to let him off the hook. "Why are you so sure Connor couldn't have done it?" she asked again.

"Just not in his nature. Was such a calm lad. Bludgeoning? Not on your life. And when I say calm, I don't mean reserved. He was a generous, open-hearted soul. Could make friends with a spider."

"You mean he wasn't calm in the sense of being repressed, or bottling up emotion," said Ruby.

Clive banged his hand on the steering wheel. "Precisely. If anyone in that family planned to stab someone, Fina is the only one with the temperament to do it."

21

Fina sat on a cold, hard bench by the front desk of the police station. Merry snowflakes outside seemed to taunt her in this rather un-Christmas-like situation. Her stomach churned and her shoulders ached. She winced as she readjusted her bruised legs. Blasted Mrs Trumper. Blasted village. Blasted police.

"Here, Miss Aubrey-Havelock. Have a cuppa. Sweet and hot." PC Budge handed her a chipped teacup with some rather dubious brown liquid in it. At least it was warm. She took a tentative sip and burned her tongue, but not before spilling it on her coat. *Sums up how this day is going.*

"Now, tell me what happened." He sat down across from her, smoothed out his trouser legs and scribbled on a pad.

"You've obviously already made up your mind. Otherwise you would have arrested Mrs Trumper."

He stared at her with cool blue eyes. She shrank back, remembering how those same eyes had bored into her when she'd answered questions about her father's murder.

The PC's eyes softened. "Mr Scammel told me – reluctantly, I should add – you were the one who began the assault, even if Mrs Trumper participated."

The clock in the corner with a crack in the glass ticked. Incessantly. It was the same clock that had been there before. She stared at PC Budge's shoelaces. One was untied. And the other was tied too tight. It appeared to be strangling his foot.

"Miss Aubrey-Havelock?"

Fina levelled her best glazed-eyed stare at him. "Strictly speaking, she's the one who started it ten years ago, when she assaulted Connor with the same handbag."

PC Budge stiffened as she said her brother's name. He folded over the top of the writing pad and scratched his head. "Is that what this is all about? My goodness, you Aubrey-Havelocks don't forget, do you?"

"What do you mean, we don't forget?"

PC Budge leaned back in his swivel chair and sucked on his pencil. "I'm not sure what I meant."

Fina suddenly forgot everything about her current predicament. She leaned forward, gaining the upper hand – at least temporarily – in this conversation. "Do you mean that our family has photographic memories?"

"Well, yes, now that you mention it. Your brother did. I remember that we asked him about all sorts of documents and photos and he could describe them without any effort."

"Such as?"

"Ticket stubs, railway tickets, bank statements, account ledgers, photos ... anything we asked him about."

"Why are you telling me this?" Her voice broke, and the tears welled up. It was partially strategic but she felt like crying anyway so it wasn't that difficult.

PC Budge's eyes flashed. Just for a moment, Fina caught a look of guilt passing over his face. His body crumpled.

"Have you been holding onto something about my father's murder?" She wiped away a tear.

PC Budge rummaged around in his pocket and withdrew a handkerchief that resembled a rat's tail.

Fina waved away his offering. Then she stamped one foot. "Tell me, you blithering idiot. You'd better tell me. Or I'll make your Christmas a living hell. I promise you. I'll assault every person who ever did me wrong in this village. And I can tell you there are quite a few since I found out what loyalty really means after the murder trial."

The pencil fell from between his pursed lips. "Right. Now I'll write you up for verbally assaulting a police officer." He fumbled around for his pencil, nearly turning over his chair.

Fina sighed and held up a placating hand. "I'm sorry. I shouldn't have called you a blithering idiot. That wasn't very sporting of me. But my threat to make your Christmas a living hell is a standing offer. I have little to lose, after all."

He sighed and wagged a finger at her. "If you tell anyone else, God curse you." He leaned forward in a conspiratorial way, although they were the only two people in the station. "Since the execution – not the trial, mind you – I've had my doubts. The reason is that no one actually saw your brother go into the honey shop. And although he may have been angry with your father, he'd nothing like what you'd call a motive. And that's when I wondered. He remembered everything, your brother, absolutely everything.

"And remembering everyone's secrets, even when you don't know they're secrets, can be most dangerous."

22

Clive Studmarsh's red Singer skidded to a halt in front of the small, squat police station in the heart of the village. Out stepped Clive, Pixley and Ruby, picking their way onto the road, which was now covered in patches of ice. The temperature had dropped rapidly in the past hour.

Clive pulled up his collar. "It's better if you two stay in the car – Auntie gave me cash for bail if we need it. Though I doubt we do. I think we'll get out of here more quickly if I handle it. I've known PC Budge since I was a child."

Ruby and Pixley nodded and hopped back into the car. Pixley handed Ruby another rug from the back seat. She turned around to face him. "While Clive is inside, tell me what you think of him."

"He's rather handsome, isn't he?" Pixley gave her a wry smile.

"Stop it, you oaf. You know precisely what I mean."

Pixley pulled out a woollen cap from his pocket and pulled it down over his bald head. "Not a fashion statement, but by all that's holy, I need warmth." He rubbed his hands. "Seems a nice enough chap, and his story about what happened seems plausible. The most plausible I've heard. And yet ..."

"Go on."

"You're the detective, Ruby Dove. You tell me."

"Oh, you are such an exasperating man sometimes, Mr Hayford." She smiled. "I agree with you. He's hiding something, but I haven't a clue if it has anything to do with the crime. Besides that, what's the motive for him to kill his uncle? Inheritance? Unlikely."

Pixley stuck his hand into his pocket and withdrew a few slips of paper. "Guess where I found these betting slips?"

"Now who's the detective?"

Pixley ignored the remark. "I had a poke around in Clive's greatcoat when we were at Marsden Court. There were at least ten more betting slips in the pocket, but I left them because I didn't want to be noticed. They're each for fifty pounds."

Ruby stared at the slips. "Primarily horse racing. And since he still has them and they're dated for events in the past, I suppose he lost a great deal of money. He can't make enough to cover all this simply by selling his sculptures, surely. Clive Studmarsh must be very hard-up indeed."

"But how would killing his uncle cancel his debts?"

"From everything we know about the Aubrey-Havelocks – including Fina – they're a generous bunch. If Hugh loaned Clive money and then cut him off, it might send him into enough of a rage to kill him."

Pixley considered this. "It's a good thought. Still a stretch because he doesn't seem to have much of a temper. But it's possible, if he were desperate enough."

Thud.

The sun had peeked out from behind the clouds for a moment, thawing the snow on top of the car. It slid down the windows, making the inside of the car into a claustrophobic ice house.

"I can't see anything, but I hear something."

Meeoow...

Ruby opened the car door. Outside, a shivering and wet black cat stood hunched over on the pathway.

"Oh no, come here, baby," Ruby cooed as she stepped out of the car. Pixley bent over the seat and squinted.

"What the devil are you doing with that mangy beast?"

Ruby scooped up the cat in her gloved hands and thrust it into the back seat. It hopped up next to Pixley and sat on a rug, licking its wet paw.

Pixley drew away. "You'll remember I'm not particularly fond of cats, and most definitely not wet and sickly ones." He peered at Ruby. "And neither, as a rule, are you. Is the Yuletide spirit finally getting to you?"

"I suppose so. But look at the poor thing. All wet and shivering. Let's take her back to Marsden Court."

"Her? How do you know the little blighter is a her?"

"I can tell."

"But we can't just take the animal. She probably belongs to someone."

Ruby puckered her lips. "It seems doubtful someone is caring for this cat. And if they are, they're doing a rather poor job of it. The grounds at Marsden Court are large enough she could live there and not bother anyone." She paused. "Besides. Fina will be so pleased to see a cat after her ordeal."

"Did someone say cat?"

Fina squeaked surprise and approval as soon as she saw the bedraggled feline curled up next to Pixley. Pixley frowned at the animal but didn't move. Indeed, there wasn't much space for him to move. The cat put a small paw on Pixley's leg. He grimaced.

The cat sat up and moved toward the newcomer in the car. Fina was glad to see a creature more pathetic than herself. She scooped it up and brought it up to her nose.

After indulging herself in a good cat-nuzzle, Fina glanced up to see Pixley giving Ruby a look of approval.

"What? Did you plan to have a pathetic cat prepared for my arrival?"

"Something like that," said Ruby. She grinned and stuck a hand out toward Fina. "Glad you're here, and not in there."

"What happened in there?" Pixley leaned toward Fina as Clive clambered in.

"Leave her alone, you newshound," said Ruby.

The driver's door slammed shut. Clive shivered but smiled at Ruby. Pixley rolled his eyes at Fina.

"Right. Let's return to Marsden Court. I'm freezing. And that police station drained away what little Christmas spirit I had." Clive started the engine and shifted into gear.

Fina stroked the cat as she watched the village roll by at a snail's pace. It resembled a picture postcard, but one that was too good to be true. All the petty squabbles, insecurities, and desperation hidden behind those chintz curtains. Not that the same couldn't be said about Marsden Court. Possibly even more so.

Pixley opened his mouth and then shut it. He held his hands together as if they could keep the words from tumbling forth.

As they left the village, Fina let out a stream of air that lifted her fringe and ruffled the shaggy fur of the now-purring cat. "I'll save you all from asking. Mrs Trumper is a bully of the worst sort. She'd not only yell at us as children, but she actually beat Connor with her handbag. When she entered Mr Scammel's general store and spewed filth about my family, well ... I snapped."

"Good old Red. Always ready for a fight." Clive puffed on a cigarette as he manoeuvred the wheel with one hand. Ruby gripped the door handle with one hand and clamped down on her hat with the other.

"I'm sure as God made little potatoes she deserved every-thing you gave her, Feens," said Ruby, without looking toward the back seat. Her eyes were fixed on the road as if she could control the direction of the car.

"Hear, hear." Pixley smiled at Fina. "And I hope PC Plod or whoever he was didn't give you too much trouble in there."

Fina bit her lip. "No, he didn't ... and in the end, he was help-ful. The memories were obviously painful, since he had been the one who interviewed me about the case. Ultimately, however, he wasn't responsible, since Scotland Yard stepped in." She paused as she massaged the cat's neck. "Mr Scammel provided useful gossip I'll tell you later, but PC Budge was the most helpful. He said something that puzzled me."

"Really? About your father or your brother?" Pixley moved the cat's outstretched paw from his leg and placed it onto the rug.

"About my brother. He said he felt like something wasn't right about the case. The first part was that no one actually saw Connor enter the shop. The second was that he didn't have a motive, other than being angry in the moment with my father. And the third part was the most revealing. He said Connor had a photographic memory like mine, which is a dangerous thing because you might know other people's secrets without knowing they're secrets."

Ruby's arms softened and she turned her head to face Fina. Any worries about Clive's driving disappeared. Fina knew that gleam in Ruby's eye all too well.

"Are you saying we've been thinking about this the wrong way around?" Ruby gripped the seat. "This means we ought to be searching for someone who had a grievance against your brother."

Pixley peeled off his spectacles. "Are you saying that someone killed Hugh in order to get rid of Connor?"

The car swerved. All heads turned toward Clive. "Awfully sorry," he said. "I was avoiding a mound of ice."

23

As they pulled into the main drive that circled in front of Marsden Court, Snave appeared in the doorway. His posture was the same as it always was – ramrod-straight – but his clasped hands belied his worry. Alice, in her white outfit, materialised out of the ether to provide a pristine contrast to the black back-drop of Snave's suit.

The cat, who Fina had christened Panther, sat calmly and comfortably in Fina's arms as she exited the car. Alice grinned at the cat, while Snave's face remained impassive.

Fina knew a fellow cat lover when she saw one. "Alice, would you take Panther to the kitchen and feed her some milk and scraps of liver, if we have any?"

Alice cradled the cat and surveyed Fina. "I'll do my best. Not sure how Cook feels about cats, but we're about to find out." She looked grateful for a reason to escape.

"Is something the matter?" Clive stamped his feet free of snow as he studied Snave.

"Yes, sir. Something is the matter. There's been an accident."

Fina's stomach clenched. Not again.

"What sort of accident?" Clive gritted his teeth. "Please tell us what happened, Snave. No need to play your role at a time like this."

Snave's shoulders lowered a half-inch as he nodded. "Please come into the warmth and I'll tell you what happened."

The little gathering did not need to be told twice. Pixley was already rubbing his head, clearly with the hope it would warm it. He had given his woollen hat to Fina to warm her icy fingers.

The hallway, with its faded silk tapestries and equally faded portraits, seemingly drained what little energy Fina had. She was exhausted. But the sight of her uncle running toward them snapped her out of her stupor. His hair flew every which way, making him resemble a caricature of a mad scientist even more than he had previously.

He narrowly missed ploughing into Ruby. "So sorry, Miss Pigeon."

"It's Dove, Uncle Harlan, not Pigeon," said Fina.

Ruby waved her hand. "Please, do go on, Mr Fotheringham."

"It's Millie. She's been poisoned."

For a moment the hallway whirled around Fina. She vaguely heard someone gasp, but sounds were muted and her eyesight was dim with shock. Until – *thud.*

Pixley lay on the floor. He had fainted.

Fina, Snave and Clive each grabbed hold of one extremity and lifted Pixley to a nearby bench. Ruby found a pillow and elevated his feet.

"I'll fetch some brandy," said Snave, clearly pleased to have a normal task to perform amidst the chaos.

"What do you mean, she's been poisoned?" Fina put a calming hand on her uncle's upper arm. His left hand quaked. She piloted him to a chair next to Pixley's bench.

"She's still alive, my dear," Harlan wheezed. "No, no, she's not left us yet. But I fear the worst." Before he could go on, Snave returned with two brandy snifters filled with amber liquid.

Seeing Harlan shaking on the bench, he gave one to Fina to administer to her uncle, and one to Ruby to administer to Pixley.

Fina held the glass up to Harlan's lips. After a tentative sip, he gulped it down and smacked his lips. "After your crowd left to go into the village – to retrieve you..." His eyes crinkled up with a trace of merriment at her, despite everything.

"Go on."

"Millie went to her bedroom. It's her usual habit to have a nap after lunch. I also know she takes her medicinal mistletoe tea before she falls asleep."

"Mistletoe tea? Never heard of it. Why does she take it?"

"Poor Millie has struggled with high blood pressure and poor circulation for a long time. The doctor prescribed mistletoe tea, twice a day – once in the afternoon and once before bed. Actually, I suspect it wasn't a doctor – more likely that herbalist, given your aunt's flights of fancy recently – but she took it as a medicine. It's also a sedative, which is why she would take it before her nap."

"What does this have to do with poisoning?"

Harlan held out his empty glass for Snave, who gave a little bow of understanding. He left them, in search of more liquid refreshment.

"Uncle Harlan, are you there?"

Harlan snapped back from his glassy-eyed stare to gaze at Fina. "Sorry, my dear. Sometimes I become a little distracted. Soon after your aunt finished her tea, she rang the bell for assistance. She couldn't see and also began to, well, vomit in the lavatory. Her memory had disappeared as well. She was confused about who we were and what she was doing. You can imagine how alarming it has been."

"Is she stable now? Should I see her?"

"She is asleep. That's the other peculiar effect. She would say things and then fall asleep. Mrs Pritchard was against calling a doctor. She said they were all quacks, but I insisted. Snave privately agreed with me."

A lovely melodic chime came from the front door – presumably one of Uncle Harlan's inventions.

Snave opened the door, revealing a tall man in a somewhat worse-for-wear Burberry. He removed his brown homburg and loud checked scarf as he entered, almost flinging them on Snave, as if this were his own home.

"Now, where's Lady Shillington?" His head swivelled around the room as if she could plausibly be located in the entryway.

"Follow me, please, Doctor Fowler," said Snave. He had already hung up the doctor's coat and was making his way across the hall.

Doctor Fowler flashed a look of puzzlement at the assembled crowd in the hallway. "What's the matter with him?" He pointed at Pixley.

"He's fainted, but he'll be fine, Doctor." Ruby smiled. "You'd better attend to Lady Shillington."

A groan came from Pixley, and he struggled to sit up. "What happened?"

"You fainted, Pix." Ruby rubbed his arm and offered him the brandy snifter. Pixley pushed it away. "Thanks, but no thanks. Really, though, what happened?"

"Lady Shillington has been poisoned by her mistletoe tea, but she is stable for the moment." Fina stood up and put a hand on her uncle's shoulder. "Isn't that correct, Uncle?"

Harlan nodded. Then he smacked his own head. "I forgot to tell you." He stared at the portrait of one of their ancient ancestors. The chap had on a marvellous red hat with a white feather.

"Yes, Uncle?" said Fina gently.

He smiled at her like a lost puppy. "What? Oh, sorry. I was thinking about my new radio hat invention ... I meant to tell you that someone has purloined your aunt's priceless hatpin collection."

Fina leaned back in her chair. Snave appeared, just in time, with a trayful of brandy. Normally, she wasn't fond of brandy. It always sounded better than it tasted. Much like when she had been a child and thought that pirate's rum must be the most delicious beverage ever. When she had tasted rum for the first time in the Caribbean, however, she'd been sorely disappointed.

She snapped back to reality as Ruby moved toward her uncle. "Mr Fotheringham, did you say her collection was stolen? As in vanished?"

Harlan made a little noise with his mouth and mimicked an explosion with his hands spread out. "*Poof*. Into thin air. *Vamoose*."

"It must be the same person who lifted the pearls," said Pixley.

Ruby tapped her teeth. "Someone here must be desperate for money – so much so that they'll risk ending a life. I wonder ... Mr Fotheringham, did you say she was poisoned by mistletoe tea?"

"That's correct." A voice came from the stairway.

It was Doctor Fowler. "Your aunt was poisoned by an overdose of mistletoe in her tea. I'll expect she'll recover in a few hours." His hand slid down the banister as he descended into the hallway. Snave materialised with his hat, overcoat and scarf.

"So you believe it to be an accident, Doctor?" Ruby smiled at him but Fina knew Ruby's smiles well. This one was a thinly veiled *I-don't-believe-you-for-a-moment* smile.

"Yes, ah, miss." He didn't even bother to ask her name. "I expect the cook put an overdose of the stuff in her tea. Either that or let it steep for too long so it became concentrated." He leaned over confidentially to Snave and said in a low voice, "I'd have a word with your cook. Or your maid, if she's the one who prepared it."

Snave barely nodded. Fina knew from his body language that he was gravely insulted by the doctor's suggestion.

She turned away from the scene at the door. Ruby had vanished.

"She flew up the stairs," said Pixley. "I expect she's going to your aunt's room to snoop."

"I'll join her." Fina regarded Pixley with concern. "Why don't you lie down yourself?" Then she looked at her uncle. He had already fallen asleep, sitting upright. Fina nodded at Snave to attend to him.

"That might be best. When Ruby is on the hunt, it's better if I stay out of the way." Pixley grinned. "Whereas you, dear Fina Watson, had better go and find Sherlock."

24

"Shhh..." Ruby held a finger to her lips. "She's sleeping."

Fina hadn't been inside her aunt's bedroom for many years. But when she had been a child, it had been one of her favourite places to hide when they played sardines. It never occurred to any of the seekers that another child would have the nerve to enter her aunt's room. She had been discovered once by her aunt, while she was hiding in a recess between the door and wardrobe. Lady Shillington had been so startled she hadn't even had time to deliver a scolding before Fina dashed out of the room.

Now here she was, watching her aunt sleeping in a glorious four-poster bed, which was decorated with a brightly coloured quilt. Aunt Millie was definitely slumbering: a small snore, the kind Fina imagined a squirrel would make, escaped her lips.

Everything else in the room was in order. Fina smiled at the precision with which her aunt's vanity table was arranged. Brushes and bottles stood in a tight square. The only peculiarity was an embroidered – and empty – jewel box on the table. This must be where the hatpins were kept.

Ruby's gloved hands picked up the teacup and water glass on the nightstand. She sniffed each and shook her head.

Out of the corner of her eye, Fina caught a stealthy movement. She surveyed the door. The knob turned. Slowly.

Ruby set down the glass and teacup and dashed toward Fina. They both huddled in the same recess in which Fina had hidden as a child. The difficulty was that now there were two of them, and they were both grown women. Fina's feet stuck out, giving the appearance that someone had been squashed underneath the wardrobe.

She held her breath. All they could do was watch.

A head popped around the door.

Fina saw a pinkish-mauve headscarf fall into the doorway before she could see the head. The smell of orange, cinnamon and sage floated into the room, as sweet as a lark.

Penelope Pritchard.

She moved like a cat burglar, first to the empty box, and then toward the bed. Penelope's flat, slipper-like, silvery shoes moved closer to her aunt. The bed obscured the rest of Fina's vision.

Ought they to confront her? Fina's head was twisted in such a way she couldn't see Ruby's face.

But the answer came easily enough. The slippered feet turned and stepped rapidly toward the door. Fina and Ruby sprang up as soon as she slipped out of the room.

Her aunt still snored gently. Thank goodness.

"Feens!" Ruby pointed at the nightstand.

The glass and teacup had vanished.

"Let's find her before she tries to dispose of them!" They rushed out of the room.

Everything was quiet in the corridor. Except one sound. A slithering sound.

Fina's head throbbed. Was it the snake again? She quickly realised it was Penelope's floor-length gown that was making the noise, dragging along the floor. She waved Ruby along and the two of them rounded the corner. There was Penelope, balancing the teacup and glass in one hand and the key to her room in the other.

"And just what do you think you are doing, Mrs Pritchard?" Fina put her hands on her hips for good measure. She had a little thrill of pleasure in confronting this otherworldly woman.

"I – I – I..." Penelope stammered. The teacup and glass fell to the floor. The teacup rolled onto the rug, unharmed, but the glass splintered into a million shards on the hardwood floor.

"Now look at what you've made me do." Penelope mirrored Fina's movement. Her hands were on her hips.

"What *I've* made you do?" Fina moved toward her.

Ruby put a hand on her friend's shoulder. "Feens. Not now. I need to analyse whatever was in that glass and that cup. Would you stand guard while I fetch a few things from my room?"

Crossing her arms, Fina nodded and stood in front of the spilt liquid, as if she were guarding the crown jewels. She glared at Penelope.

Penelope fumbled with the key in the lock. "Blast it." The key dropped to the floor. As she bent over to retrieve it, a slip of paper fell out of her pocket.

Fina scooped it up before Penelope could snatch it away. It was a newspaper clipping.

About Ruby Sparks.

This was all too much. "Why do you have a newspaper clipping about Ruby Sparks?" Fina burst out. "Why were you in my aunt's room, pilfering her water glass and teacup?"

Penelope rested her graceful back against the door in a gesture of resignation. "In answer to the second question, I was in your aunt's room because I care about her. I wanted to see how she was feeling. As for the glass and teacup, I thought it best to remove them in case she woke up and forgot what had happened. What if there were something in the water and she drank it again?"

It was a valid point. Fina relaxed her arms. "It is peculiar that Doctor Fowler left them there. I suppose since he thought it was the tea, he didn't worry about the water. In fact, he probably thought it was a good idea." She sighed. "But what about Ruby Sparks?"

"Well, I have to admit that I'm a bit of a sleuth myself. I saw this item about her in the newspaper this morning and cut it out. I thought I'd study it more closely. The members of the Elephant Gang are known to take up posts as servants. I thought maybe the maid, Alice, or the cook might be connected to Ruby Sparks – or might *be* Ruby Sparks."

Fina shifted from side to side. She didn't like the fact this woman was fixated on a Ruby, albeit a different Ruby.

Penelope turned the tables. "Speaking of which. What do you really know about your friend, Ruby?"

Fina was about to reply indignantly when a voice broke in. "Go on, Mrs Pritchard. You were about to accuse me of something?"

Ruby had returned with her doctor's bag.

"Oh, I, didn't mean..." trailed off Penelope, turning away from Ruby. She opened her door, finally, and slipped inside. She shut it firmly.

Ruby shrugged and smiled at Fina. She bent down, opened her bag and pulled out small bottles with droppers.

Pitter-patter.

Selkies and kelpies. It was Noodle. Did everyone in this house have to sneak around? The little blighter's face was covered in something red. Jam?

Noodle crouched down near the floor and then broke into a hop and skip.

"Please stay away, Noodle. Ruby and I have some important matters to attend to."

"Let's play happy families," the girl said.

Fina had to hand it to Noodle. The child had the gumption to ask her to play happy families after she had made her one unhappy woman with that snake.

"Not now."

The child was crestfallen, but then became distracted by Ruby's machinations on the floor. "What you doing?" She pointed a jammy finger at Ruby.

"Searching for clues." Ruby didn't look up from her task.

"What are clues?"

"Hints. Things people don't know."

"I know something nobody knows."

Fina sighed. The child clearly wasn't going to leave them alone, so she'd better play along. "What do you know, Noodle?"

"I'm not telling. It's a secret."

"Clues are secrets too, young Noodle," murmured Ruby. "You'd better tell us your clue."

"Mummy said I wasn't to tell anybody."

At the name 'Mummy', Fina became interested. She had spent many hours playing with young children when she herself was younger and knew something about the psychology of a child like the mischievous Noodle. "You're pulling our leg. No such secret exists."

Fina turned her back on Noodle and peered at the liquid on the floor. Though Ruby was lost in a chemistry manual, the corner of her mouth lifted in a grin.

Noodle stamped her foot. "I know a secret. A great, whopping secret." She spread out her arms as if she were a hawk about to take flight.

"No you don't."

"I do, I do, I do," Noodle squealed in frustration. "Mummy

said I could play with her pink pearls. That I could put them on my stuffed rabbit. He has a big belly and a cottontail. His name is Carrot."

"How original." Fina studied the girl. As she expected, Noodle looked puzzled by her sarcasm. Just as well. "Why would your mummy allow you to play with something that's so important to her?"

Noodle shrugged. "She said she had others."

25

"Noodle! Leave those ladies alone." Felicity, Countess of Chiverton, marched up to the little party on the landing. "You're absolutely filthy. Come, let's wash up." Felicity's mouth was set in a grim line, as if she had been enduring some awful trial. She held out her hand to her child but when Noodle stuck out her hand to clasp it, Felicity drew away. She waved at Noodle to follow.

Ruby and Fina stood up, watching mother and daughter retreat. "Are you thinking what I'm thinking?" Ruby snapped shut her doctor's bag.

"That those pearls were fake? Otherwise, why would she let Noodle play with them?"

"Precisely. It's possible she has a set of fake pink pearls for Noodle." Ruby tailed off, lost in thought.

"Did you find out anything about the liquid in the water glass?"

Ruby held up a small slip of paper with a wet, purplish stain on it. "Yes. There was mistletoe in the teacup, but not enough to do her any harm. As we suspected, there was something in the water glass."

"What was it?"

"Hyoscine."

"What's that?" Pixley lumbered up to them, hands in pockets.

"It's a poison that mimics the effects of mistletoe. But it's much deadlier."

Pixley took off his spectacles and rubbed them with a handkerchief. "Come again? I can't take this in."

"I believe your aunt might be in danger." Ruby walked toward Lady Shillington's room. "We shouldn't leave her unattended."

As they rounded the corner, they spied Alice turning the knob on the door to Lady Shillington's room. She balanced a tea tray in one hand.

"What are you doing, Alice?"

"Bringing Lady Shillington some tea, miss. Mrs Standish told me it would cheer her up."

"Why is Mrs Standish giving you orders?" Fina held the tray so Alice could finish opening the door.

"It's not as peculiar as it seems, miss. I was passing her in the hallway and she enquired after Lady's Shillington's health. Everyone is in a state downstairs. After I told her she was resting, Mrs Standish said I ought to bring up her own pot of tea as she didn't want it."

Ruby gently lifted the tray away from Fina. "Let's not give anything to Lady Shillington at the moment, shall we? I believe she is in grave danger, Alice."

Alice's mouth formed a little 'o', which she tried to hide with one hand. "I'm ever so sorry, Miss. I thought it was just an accident with the tea. Mr Snave was bitter as bile when he scolded the cook and me."

"It wasn't your fault. It wasn't Cook's fault, either. Someone deliberately slipped poison into Lady Shillington's water glass."

Alice wrapped her apron around her finger. She was either a

very good actor, or she was genuinely terrified. "Poison? But Doctor Fowler said she'd be right as rain. Is she going to die?"

"Doctor Fowler didn't examine her water glass. And no, she won't die. I expect she'll be asleep for a few more hours, but she ought to be fine by this evening. But in the meantime, I'd like to ask you to keep watch by her door. Let no one in, except Mr Fotheringham and Snave. Understood?"

Alice demonstrated her agreement by sitting down on a mahogany chair next to the door. She appeared relieved to be seated. "The only trouble is that we're short on staff. And the snow is coming down a treat. I won't wonder if we're not cut off by nightfall."

PIXLEY HELD up a sketch of what appeared to be Gerald Standish, dressed in Napoleon's clothes. "Rather natty, if I say so myself." He peered at the page.

The trio sat in the study – a pleasingly square room, filled with just the right number of books and just the right size furniture. Panther sat on Fina's lap, licking a glossy black paw. Cook had taken quite a shine to the cat and had not only fed her well but groomed her, too.

Ruby flipped through the sketchbook. "I didn't realise you could draw. Impressive talent, Mr Hayford." She gave out one of her rare belly laughs as she flipped the page then handed the sketchbook to Fina. "Look at Lord Chiverton."

Fina laughed. Basil Thynne was pointing a stick at a blackboard as he instructed a group of serious young mice.

"I took up sketching after our trip on the *Train Blanc*." Pixley stretched out his short legs far enough to reach the fire. "And I found it useful for my job as a journalist, too. It helps me remember personalities."

"Speaking of personalities," said Ruby in a low warning voice, "have you heard from that personality named Mr Ian Clavering?"

Pixley held up a hand. "Afraid not. The Arbuthnots must be keeping him busy. No doubt he's suffering through endless rounds of charades. Why, were you expecting him to ring?"

"Not a bit of it! Good riddance to bad rubbish." Ruby swished her hands against each other as if she were finished with Ian Clavering forever.

Fina patted Panther's head. It was time to change the subject. "Do you have a sketch of everyone at Marsden Court, Pix?"

"Just about. Except for young Noodle. I'm unable to capture the essence of children – yet. Though I expect I could draw her pulling at Panther's tail." He took the notebook from Fina and tore out each page. "I thought we could use these to review our list of suspects."

Ruby sipped her tea. She was calm, save a slight twitch at one corner of her mouth. "Suspects for which case?"

"Precisely. That's the problem. We've got so many cases, I can't keep track."

"I'll be scribe! That's what I'm best at." Fina leaned over to her handbag, doing her best not to disturb the cat. Panther's tail flicked with annoyance. Fina slid her hand inside the bag. She had cleaned it out yesterday so it didn't take long for her to find her notebook and pen.

But then her hand brushed across something else. Something that certainly hadn't been there yesterday.

It was a folded piece of paper.

26

Fina held up one finger to quiet Pixley and Ruby's chattering. "Look. Someone left me a note." She unfolded the scrap of paper. The brown, grainy quality reminded her of something. Newsprint. Sure enough, there were printed words around the edges of the empty space. Though it was no longer empty. Someone had scrawled: '*Bruno Daniels is not what he seems.*'

Pixley snatched the newsprint and read it again, out loud, and slowly. He pushed his spectacles up the bridge of his nose. "Well, well. This might make a good story."

Ruby grabbed the paper from Pixley. "Please put away your journalist hat. Time to remain focused on our cases. Now, why would someone put this in your bag? And why does it appear to be a child's handwriting?"

"Maybe this was Noodle's real secret." Fina smiled. Then she frowned. "Joshing aside, it looks as though someone were trying hard to make the script resemble scrawl. Why would they slip it in my bag and why should they think I'd care about Bruno Daniels?"

"Everyone here is aware of your family's case. That's the only reason I can see to put it in your handbag. It cannot have anything to do with the thefts because there's no reason they'd give it to you, specifically, and there's no indication this has anything to do with the theft." Pixley sat back in the plush sofa and arranged his fingers into a steeple gesture.

"Do you think Bruno is hard up? That could be why he stole the pearls. Assuming he thought the pearls were real – and that they are, indeed, real." Fina stroked Panther in a rhythmic motion.

"I doubt it," said Ruby. "This has something to do with the murder. Let's incorporate this clue into our review, shall we?" She bounced out of her seat and began to arrange Pixley's portraits of the guests on the fireplace mantel. Pixley trundled to the door of the study and locked it. "Just in case," he said, more to himself than to Ruby and Fina.

"Let's begin with the hardest case, which is your family. We can discuss the pearl theft motives, too." Ruby's voice trailed off. Then she squared her shoulders and pointed at the first portrait, of her cousin, Clive. Pixley had drawn him sculpting a horse.

"I've brought out his artistic good looks," said Pixley, winking at Fina.

Ruby let out an exaggerated sigh. Ignoring Pixley, she said, "Clive Studmarsh had opportunity to commit the murder. We don't know of any motive other than he is always hard up for money. And a chronic gambler, as well as a starving artist. He's likely in debt to some loan shark he pays every month. I don't see how murdering your father would solve any of these problems. Though he had a motive to steal those pearls. And the hatpins."

"I think my father lent him money from time to time. The Aubrey-Havelocks are a generous lot. I suppose something could have gone pear-shaped around money. As for murdering my father to frame my brother, I cannot see anything past the same money motive – though how would framing my brother solve any of that?"

"Did Clive and Connor get on?" Pixley poured himself a glass of scotch and swished it as if it were a glass of brandy.

"Yes and no. They were both easy-going, popular, and friendly. Though they were friends with each other, sometimes I think their charm created a little competition between them. Clive saved Connor's life once. That's how he came by that scar near his eyebrow."

"So Connor was in Clive's debt," murmured Pixley. "Owed him his life. That's an interesting dynamic. Can often lead to trouble..."

Ruby nodded. "Let's move on to your uncle. Uncle Harlan." She pointed a finger at the mad-scientist-like portrait.

"Uncle Harlan?" Fina straightened up. "Surely you cannot suspect him of anything." She paused, seeing Ruby's sympathetic but steady gaze. "I suppose everyone has to be a suspect. Uncle Harlan isn't really my uncle – not a blood relation, at least. He's always been one to live in his own world. I believe there was a love interest between he and my aunt at some point."

Pixley leaned forward and licked his lips.

"You are incorrigible, Mr Hayford," giggled Fina. "Even if they'd had a passionate love affair, I cannot see what it has to do with my father and brother."

"If he married your aunt, would he gain a lot of money?" Ruby began to pace in small irregular circles around the fireplace poker and bellows.

"I suppose, but it's unnecessary since he lives here anyway. I suspect my aunt gives him an allowance."

"Did he get on with your father and brother?"

Fina paused. "He had a few blazing rows with my father. Spectacular, really. I cannot remember what they were about, but Harlan has a temper. He controls it most of the time under his absent-minded façade, but there's something hard underneath. As for my brother, he was always kind to him."

"How about the earl and countess?" Pixley popped up to admire his own handiwork. "They make my skin crawl."

"They certainly had a money motive. Not to mention that Felicity was seen going into my father's shop that day."

"Why would she have a reason to enter the shop?"

"At the trial, she said it was to discuss the school." Fina paused.

"But you think otherwise?" Ruby leaned forward.

Fina blew a puff of air upward toward her fringe. "It's just that since we've been here, her strange behaviour – not to mention Basil's vice-like grip on her – gives me to wonder whether..."

"She might have had more personal reasons for the visit?"

"Mmmh ... Not that my father reciprocated, of course."

Tap, tap.

"Telephone, Mr Hayford."

27

Snave's eyes flickered momentarily as he stared at the sketches on the mantel.

"Right you are, Snave." Pixley turned to Ruby and Fina. "Carry on. I won't be long."

"Who knows Pixley is here? You don't think someone outside Marsden Court is aware of the theft or the poisoning?" Fina's stomach clenched.

"No need to worry for the moment, Feens. Let's think about the Standishes for now. Marjorie flings herself at men, so I suppose that could be some sort of love interest between her and your father or brother. Sorry to have to mention it."

"Not at all." Though a little stab of pain arose in her stomach with her friend's words, the ache was not as strong as it would have been even a few months ago. She took a moment to reflect and then returned to the discussion. "Although, objectively speaking, it seems unlikely. I'm sure I heard something about Marjorie recently – something pointing in quite a different direction. Now what was it?"

While she pondered, Ruby ploughed on. "As for Gerald, it could be some old boyhood grudge. But again, money seems a more plausible motive. It could be some business problem from before. Though it seems like that would have been resolved a while ago."

"What about Bruno? Do you think the note is somehow connected to my father?"

Sparks flew out of the fireplace, followed by a loud popping noise that made Ruby jump. "Could be."

Fina continued. "So let's say he's a fraud and my father or brother knew about it. Maybe he was afraid one or both of them would expose him?"

"Plausible. Might be a definitive motive for your father's case."

"That about wraps up the suspects." Fina put down her pen and stroked Panther. Then she thought she could do with tea and lovely chocolate biscuits.

As if she were a mind-reader, Ruby bent down over a side table near the teapot. She held a tray of precious cargo aloft. "Behold! Chocolate biscuits! Looks like your energy is flagging, Feens."

Panther glared up in annoyance as crumbs tumbled onto her head. "Sorry, Panther." Fina brushed away the crumbs. "Selkies and kelpies." She held up a finger. "We're forgetting one person. Penelope Pritchard."

"I thought you'd never seen her before." Ruby leaned against the fireplace, nibbling on her own biscuit.

"Yes, but what if there's a connection between Edward Pritchard – her husband – and my father's death?"

"Seems far-fetched. But anything is possible, as we know too well."

Fina took up her pen again and put a question mark next to Penelope's name.

The door flew open. Small beads of sweat lined the crown of Pixley's bald head.

"I had to come back here before they roped me in, too. Is there somewhere I can hide?"

"Pixley Hayford. Are you off your onion?" Fina wagged a finger streaked with chocolate at him. "Your need for the dramatic will come back to haunt you some day."

Pixley pushed his spectacles back on his nose, this time so far that they magnified his eyes. "You're quite right. I'm shameless. The atmosphere must be getting to me. Everyone is, well, becoming a bit delirious. They're playing games in the winter garden."

"What kind of games?"

"I wouldn't be surprised if those wretched twins slipped something into everyone's tea or afternoon drinks, the way they're carrying on." He waved them out of the study. "You must witness this for yourselves."

They tiptoed through the musty hallway. After a few twists and turns, they arrived at the fecund-smelling door of the glassed-in winter garden. Pixley opened the opaque wooden door a crack and pointed at Fina. She crept forward – there was only enough room for one person at a time to peek in.

Snow was piled high on either side of the glass enclosure, creating a snug and secure effect, while white dots pattered on the top and sides of the structure. It was twilight, so everything had taken on a blueish tinge from the snow. Potted orange and lemon trees, bearing fruit, lined the side of the room. They reminded Fina of those jars of orange and yellow hard sweets in Mr Scammel's shop.

The centre of the room, however, held her attention much more than these decorative details. Clive, Gerald, Marjorie, Penelope, Cecily, Celestia, Bruno and Harlan were all on their knees in a semi-circle. Everyone was laughing so hard they had to take in deep breaths in between bursts of giggles.

Cecily – or was it Celestia? – had a small red-and-white box stuck on her nose. It was a box of safety matches. The redhead squealed with delight as if she were as happy as a pig in muck.

She bent over toward Gerald on her left, whose forehead was creased from laughter. He moved closer to Cecily as she tried to transfer the matchbox to Gerald's nose, while her hands were clasped behind her back. Marjorie, kneeling next to Gerald, stopped laughing. She was the only one. In order to transfer the box, Gerald and Cecily had to rub noses.

The red-and-white box tumbled to the floor. Fina jumped from the uproarious shriek of laughter from the crowd. Everyone fell over on their sides, laughing.

Celestia dusted off her frock and stood up. "Now we shall play rabbit's kiss!"

Ruby tapped her on the shoulder. "Feens," she hissed. "Let me have a peek."

Fina moved out of the way and sat down on a bench next to Pixley. "What the devil is going on in there? And my uncle! And Penelope!"

"It's difficult for me to believe it's the strain causing them to do this," sighed Pixley. "The twins must be at it again with their drugs. Who knows what kind of concoction they've mixed this time."

Fina smiled. "But it provides us with a convenient opportunity to snoop."

28

Ruby giggled. Without turning around, she waved at Fina and Pixley.

Fina knelt down and squeezed her head below Ruby's so she could see, too.

Celestia was standing with her hands behind her back and a long thread hanging out of her mouth. She paced back and forth.

She mumbled between her teeth, "Who's next?"

Bruno and Marjorie stepped forward, knocking into one another. Bruno said, "Ladies first."

Marjorie glared at him but took him up on his offer. Penelope gasped. So did Gerald. Harlan tittered. Cecily's eyes crinkled from the wide smile on her mouth. Clive slapped his knees with delight.

Cecily reached into her handbag and removed a tin of silk dental floss. She unfurled a generous length of it and placed it between Marjorie's teeth.

Bruno leaned over with his hands behind his back and grabbed at the cotton thread with his lips. After fumbling about for a minute, like a fish aimlessly opening its mouth in a feeding frenzy, he finally clenched it between his teeth.

Once the string was taut, the pair chewed on the silk floss, coming closer and closer until they were in a kiss. And it wasn't just any kiss.

Silence.

Silence until Fina lost her balance and tumbled in through the door.

Marjorie screamed. As soon as Fina had fallen, she tripped Ruby up and the two of them sat on the floor, rubbing their heads after bumping them on the doorframe.

Clive laughed. Cecily joined in. Soon everyone was doubled over laughing.

Ruby smoothed her hair. "This place is a den of iniquity, as my grandmother would say. Time to leave."

The pair scrambled to their feet, dashed out of the winter garden and slammed the door shut, as if they were trying to wake from a nightmare.

"You two are the cat's whiskers." Pixley chuckled and turned on his heel. "Are you coming? Let's search while those cuckoo birds are still in a state of ecstasy."

Fina blew a puff of air at her fringe. "I need more chocolate. And fast."

Ruby shot Pixley a knowing glance. "I'll wager we'll find a box of chocolates in someone's room. I'm sure they won't mind if we swipe one or two."

Fina's spirits rose. "You're on." She shot off toward the stairs, faster than thought or time.

She halted. And sniffed. What was that smell?

"What is it, Feens?"

"Can you smell that? It's my father's aftershave. He didn't wear it often. But it's very distinctive. My mother used to buy it for him every Christmas. It was specially made for him, so that's why it stopped me in my tracks."

Fina took a delicate step to her left, to her front, and then back. "It's vanished. But it was definitely there."

"Perhaps it's just your memory that's tricking you?" Pixley stepped forward and put a hand on her shoulder.

Fina dropped her shoulder and turned away. "Are you doubting me?"

Ruby said, "I'm certain he's not, but it is true that one memory might suggest another. I've had it happen to me before."

"Perhaps, but I swear it was real. I'm certain as spring softness follows winter's ice."

"What do you swear there was? Blasphemy, my dear." Basil Thynne made a 'tsk' noise with his teeth on the stairs.

"Oh, I thought I smelled my father's aftershave. I'm sure you'd recognise it too, Lord Chiverton. Do you?"

He took the slightest step backward on the stairs, almost causing him to fall over. "No, no." He moved back. "Excuse me, I forgot something in my room." Then he turned and fled.

"Interesting." Ruby sniffed the air again. "Your nose might be correct."

"Only one way to find out." Pixley lifted his legs up the stairs as if he were climbing Everest. "Let's split up and snoop."

"Is that wise? And how do we know what we're looking for – besides the pearls, hatpins, and anything of interest to my father's case? And isn't it a little dangerous?" Fina had a rising sense of panic as she listed all the things they had to account for at once.

"We'll meet in Fina's room in twenty minutes." Ruby surveyed her watch. "That's five o'clock. If one of us doesn't show up, then the other two will start searching for them. Pixley, why don't you take the downstairs? I'll take the first floor and Feens can take the second."

"And how do I explain myself if someone comes in while I'm searching?" Pixley descended the stairs.

"You'll come up with something, Pix. You're a journalist."

29

Fina started with the twins' room. They insisted on sharing, as they did with everything else. There was something decidedly shifty about the twins – something other than their passion for mind-altering substances.

Rather appropriately, Lady Shillington had placed the twins in the Red Room. After finding the extra skeleton keys in the kitchen, Fina had distributed them to Ruby and Pixley. The keys clinked together in a merry jingling noise as Fina fumbled to find the correct one for this lock. Finally, a satisfying *click* came from the door to the Red Room.

The door creaked as it opened. The interior of the room resembled the morning after a sea squall. Beautiful sparkly clothes were draped here and there, creating a disorienting effect as Fina lifted piles of toiletries and frocks in an effort to make sense of the mess.

She peeked in the jewellery box on the tallboy.

Pink pearls.

Fina slipped them out of the box. She wracked her brain, trying to recall what some debutante had told her once about how to tell if they were genuine. Gingerly, she rubbed one bead against her front teeth. It was smooth. No grit. They might be genuine, but it seemed unlikely the twins would leave stolen pearls unattended in their own jewellery box. Then again, they had been drug-addled almost the entire weekend, so anything was possible. Still, she curled them into her pocket. Only until they could sort it all out.

She sighed and turned round the room like a searchlight.

Her heart stopped. An ivory shoe protruded from underneath the bed, just visible where the hem of the eiderdown didn't quite reach to the floor.

"Selkies and kelpies," Fina whispered to herself. She knelt down beside the bed. Grabbing the bedclothes, she pulled them upwards.

Her hand flew to her chest as the shoe proclaimed itself to be empty.

Curiosity soon replaced relief. Underneath the shoe sat a piece of newsprint. She tugged at it, revealing a bundle of newspapers. The first was the *Daily Worker*, a newspaper for communists. The headline read, '*Blackshirts Outnumbered by Working-Class Party*'. The second was the *Black Star*, for anarchists. The headline read, '*Emma Goldman Speaks*'. And the third was the *Irish Worker*, an anti-imperialist socialist newspaper. The headline read '*Confirmed. British Infiltration of Irish Workers Party*'.

Fina let out a low whistle. This was the last thing she'd expected of the twins. Perhaps someone had given the papers to them and they took them out of politeness? It would certainly explain how all this had ended up under the bed instead of on the desk.

Light, rapid footsteps came from the hallway. At first, Fina thought it might be Noodle. Then she realised there were two people. The footsteps stopped in front of the door.

She dived beneath the bed, only to find it was scarcely large enough for her to squeeze under. Sucking in her gut, she wriggled underneath.

The twins breezed in, laughing and chatting. "Darling, did you see their faces? It was too, too precious. Now. What did you do with the pearls?"

The other said, "I put them in the jewellery box, sweetie."

"But they're not here."

There was a silence. To Fina, struggling to suppress an itch in her nose, it seemed to last far beyond the time it would normally take two people to exchange startled glances. Finally, a knock came at the door. Fina heard it open and then one of the twins began to positively purr. "Bruno, darling, what are you doing here?"

"Ah, I thought, well, the three of us..."

Fina didn't have to see Bruno to know he was leering at the twins. So scandalised by whatever it was he was suggesting, she temporarily forgot her plight.

And then she sneezed.

"Bless you."

"I didn't sneeze, and neither did Bruno."

Footsteps approached the bed. Fina could see a pair of black velvet heels halt in front of her.

She held her breath. A nail or splinter of wood jutted into her back. If she moved farther underneath, it would certainly dig into her skin. She must wriggle closer to the centre of the bed.

But there wasn't only one nail, there were two.

"Eeee!" she yelped.

Now two other pairs of footsteps approached the bed. A hand lifted the valance. Bruno's head peered underneath, as if he were seeking buried treasure.

"Hullo, hullo, Miss Aubrey-Havelock."

Fina gulped. She couldn't even slide out from underneath the bed because that blasted nail had snagged her frock.

"Aren't you going to come out and explain yourself?" One twin popped into sight next to Bruno's head.

"I cannot." She cursed the feebleness of her own voice. "My frock is caught on a nail."

Next thing she knew, Bruno had grabbed hold of her hands and yanked her forward. She heard a tearing noise, followed by her own yelp.

But it had worked. She was now lying in a heap on the floor, much like the heaps of clothing strewn about the room.

Fina blinked at the bright light as if she were a vampire who had been rudely awakened during the day.

Both twins loomed over her, hands on their hips. "Well. You'd better explain yourself."

The other added, "And quickly."

Despite her position, Fina was distracted by this hard edge to the twins. She hadn't seen this before. Though to get to this position in life, she supposed, they probably had to be tough as boots.

Bruno stood by, leaning on one of the four posters, smoking a cigarette. He appeared amused, and not at all shocked.

In an effort to hoist herself up, Fina planted her hands next to her, but slipped. Her palms were clammy. Instead, she leaned back on her arms, trying to appear casual, as if being found underneath a guest's bed were an everyday occurrence at Marsden Court.

"You look rather smug. I cannot understand why." One of the twins lit up a cigarette and blew a stream of smoke down at Fina.

"Excuse me."

A voice came from the doorway and everyone spun around. Except for Fina, who reclined even further and grinned.

30

"What are *you* doing here?" One twin tapped her foot.

Ruby and Pixley stood in, or rather blocked, the doorway.

"There you are, Fina," said Ruby, ignoring the twin's question. Without invitation, Pixley stepped toward Fina. He lifted her up in one deft movement, made possible by his 'bulging biceps', as Fina called them when she wanted to tease him.

While Pixley helped Fina to her feet, Ruby smoothed her hair. "I apologise, but you two ought to be more careful with your recreational beverages. Fina has had this kind of paranoid reaction once before. Remember, Feens? In Barcelona?"

Barcelona? Fina's brain did feel as if it had been subjected to a mind-altering substance. But one that induced a muddled brain rather than paranoia.

Pixley nodded his head so rapidly his spectacles threatened to fly onto the floor. "Oh yes. It was quite a sight. Perhaps Fina doesn't remember. We found her underneath the bed of a royal guest at the hotel. Paranoid and squiffy." He laughed. "Rather challenging to explain the pos-ish to the Prince."

Pos-ish? Why was Pixley speaking like Bertie Wooster? Must be his nerves.

The twins' mouths snapped shut, as if they were trying to keep a secret. Bruno's eyes slid from Pixley, to Fina, and then to Ruby. He took a final puff on his cigarette and smashed it in a glass ashtray he held in his hand. "Seems a plausible explanation. I had a bad reaction once. Though it was to a mushroom. I never take drugs recreationally, of course. It wouldn't do for a member of parliament."

As shameless as a pig. Lord Strathclyde was certainly a smooth customer – a phrase Fina had picked up at the pictures. He was attempting to divert attention from the fact that Fina had heard his proposition to the twins.

Pixley, ever the man of action, piloted Fina to the doorway. "Right-ho, all, we'll be seeing you. Must get Fina into a cold bath."

ONCE IN THE HALLWAY, Fina doubled over in uncontrollable laughter. "You two were marvellous. I had no idea how to escape that situation. Though Pixley needs to cut down on his consumption of Wodehouse."

"Did you find out anything useful?" Ruby sat down on a bench in the hallway, away from the sight of the twins' room.

Fina pulled out the strand of pearls from her frock.

Pixley's eyes gleamed. "Nice one. I suppose it was worth it." He took the pearls and scraped the beads against his teeth. "As we suspected, these are fake. It could be they're the twins' pearls but then Felicity's originals could have been paste."

"As Noodle suggested," said Fina as she patted down her hair. She leaned over and waved Ruby and Pixley closer. "Two more items of interest. One is the twins had communist, socialist, and anarchist literature – poking out from underneath the bed. And another thing. I think Bruno was propositioning the twins."

"Well, well," said Pixley. "I'd expect nothing less from him, as a member of parliament. Goes with the territory."

"Yes, but it's also a motive to silence someone – like Connor, or my father?"

Pixley and Ruby nodded slowly, mulling things over.

"But it seems a far-fetched idea. Why would your father or Connor know of his dangerous liaisons?" Pixley wiggled his eyebrows provocatively.

Fina sighed. "Yes, I suppose it is rather improbable."

Ruby smiled at Fina. "Not all is lost. As for the political literature, it's interesting. The fact that it was on the floor suggests it's not significant. But still." She tapped her teeth.

"Did you two find out anything?"

Pixley shook his head. "I searched Bruno's room and it was remarkably neat and tidy. Nothing of interest that I could find."

"Why do you say remarkably?" Ruby smoothed her skirt.

"Bruno strikes me as a man of outsized appetites – in all areas of life. In my experience with that type of personality, they are enjoying so much that they have little time for mundane details such as keeping their shoes in a perfect line."

"I searched Penelope's room, which was more like the twins' in terms of disorder. It made it a little more difficult to find anything. But I found her bank book. There were several cheques from Lady Shillington to Penelope, written on a regular basis."

"What does that mean?" Pixley tapped his foot. "That she pays Penelope a regular allowance? Surely you don't think it's extortion." He paused. "Or do you?"

Ruby had that far-off look in her eye. Lost in those remarkable webs of her brain.

Fina heard footsteps. Through the slats in the banister lining the square-circle of the interior of the house, she glimpsed a small figure skipping along.

"Hurry," said Fina as she popped up from the bench. "Dreadful Noodle is skipping toward us like a runaway train. Let's find refuge in my room."

"Why is your door open?" Pixley pointed at the Green Room's door, which was open just enough to let a sliver of light pour out.

Fina patted her pockets to check for her key. "That's odd. I'm sure I locked it."

"I'm sorry, Feens, but you seem particularly accident-prone today. Let me go first." Ruby pushed on the door. Pixley and Fina stood behind, ready to enter. But before they could even peer past Ruby, the silence was broken with a shriek.

31

With a gasp, Fina fell back. Pixley, though, didn't hesitate. Snatching the first makeshift weapon that came to hand – a plaster bust of Alfred, Lord Tennyson, which had been resting on a deal table in the hall – he burst through Fina's door. Alfred did not appear pleased to be disturbed.

"So sorry, dear." Lady Shillington sat in front of them. "I gave poor Miss Dove a fright when I turned around in this high-backed chair. It was inconsiderate of me. Please accept my apologies."

Ruby nodded, still clutching her chest.

Fina touched her aunt's hand as if she were an apparition. "Aunt Millie, thank goodness you're all right! What on earth are you doing here? How did you escape your room if Alice was guarding the door? And aren't you too sick to even be moving about?"

"So many questions, dear Red. But that was you as a child, too. Always asking questions." She smiled at Fina fondly. "I convinced Alice that I had partially recovered and told her I had business to attend to with you."

"Did you just wake up and feel better?" Pixley descended into a settee as if he were a creaky lift.

Lady Shillington gifted them a wry smile. "I wasn't feeling poorly to begin with, dear boy. Unfortunately, I had to deceive you all to protect myself. And most likely to protect Red, as well."

Unlike Fina and Pixley, who had almost disappeared into the plush cushions arranged around the room, Ruby was invigorated. There was long oval rug in front of Fina's fireplace, ideal for Ruby's pacing habit. And she made good use of it. "You believe someone in this house wants to kill you, don't you?"

"Oh, it's more than intuition, let me assure you," Lady Shillington leaned on a walking stick she had with her. Fina had never seen it before. "This walking stick is for protection – I see your puzzled look, Red. You see, when I lay down for my habitual nap this afternoon, Alice brought me my mistletoe tea, prepared by Cook."

"Who is aware of your mistletoe tea habit?" Pixley tapped his pipe into a nearby ashtray.

"Well, quite naturally everyone in the household. As for the guests, everyone else knows as well because Penelope and I were chatting about it during lunch. The guests became fascinated by it, I suppose, because they had heard mistletoe tea was poisonous. Penelope, who was the one who recommended I take it in the first place for my high blood pressure, explained that in small quantities it was actually beneficial. Gerald was adamant that this didn't make any sense. He believes Penelope's herbalism is a lot of bosh. But when she pointed out that digitalis is poisonous in large quantities – even though it's a heart medicine – everyone went as quiet as the grave."

Ruby ignored Lady Shillington's unfortunate idiom. "Did anyone change the conversation at that point?"

Lady Shillington's face twisted as she contemplated the

question. "Now you mention it, it was Felicity who changed the subject rather abruptly. Surely, though, she was only trying to avoid an awkward silence."

Ruby said nothing as she stared at her own shoes. "Please go on, Lady Shillington."

"I lay down for my nap. Alice brought me my tea. I drank it. It didn't taste peculiar, overly bitter, or like bitter almonds – as they say in detective novels. I know that because when I first asked Mrs Bramble to brew the tea, she made it a little too strong. It's too bitter to drink when that happens. I was thirsty, so I poured a glass of water from the jug. It was just enough for one glass."

"Someone must have drained it so there wouldn't be evidence that remained." Fina felt pleased by her deduction, despite the generalised chaos of her brain at the moment.

"Precisely." Her aunt made a little whipping gesture with her forefinger in Fina's direction. "I was about to sip from the glass, when I noticed there was a sheen on the top of the water. Similar to the little clouds of oil that form on the surface of soup. I then examined the surface of the water in the jug and it was clean."

Pixley leaned forward. "So someone put the poison – or whatever it was—"

"Hyoscine," Ruby interjected.

"Quite. They put it in the bottom of the glass. Clever."

"Yes, Mr Hayford, that is what I thought. I knew this couldn't be an accident. And then I thought I'd play the role I was supposed to play."

"Why didn't you tell us all about it?" Fina was beginning to realise she had underestimated her aunt.

"To be honest, dear Red, I was going to do that at first. But then I ruminated over it. You see, most of the guests – including the family – have been acting rather peculiarly around me. Mind you, I've been asking questions."

Fina's heart raced. "About what?"

Lady Shillington leaned in and lowered her voice.

"About your father's murder."

32

Eyes cast down, Lady Shillington went on: "It's only been during the past few months I've been able to grieve. Dear Penelope has been so helpful in that – helping me with her herbs."

Pixley choked on his glass of water. "So sorry, Lady Shillington. Please ignore me."

She gave him a crooked smile. "I know you all think it's a lot of tommyrot, but I feel much improved. I wanted find out more about what happened because I simply couldn't believe Connor killed Hugh."

"Neither could I," said Fina. "But you already knew that."

"Wait." Ruby halted at the exact centre of the rug. "Did you invite this, how shall I say it, rather eclectic group of guests here for a purpose? To find out what really happened?"

"I see now why you and Red are such good friends, Miss Dove. Smart as a whip." She sighed and leaned on her walking stick again. "Yes, I thought that somehow, almost by magic, if I brought together everyone who was involved in that crime, then I would find out what happened. I admit it was rather foolish."

"On the contrary, Lady Shillington." Pixley put his hand casually across the back of the sofa. "From a journalist's perspective, it makes perfect sense. Gather everyone together. Observe. Ask questions and see what happens."

Lady Shillington sighed. "Thank you, young man. But it's all gone rather pear-shaped, as you young people say."

"Pixley's right." Fina leaned forward and blew a puff of air into her fringe. "You've clearly hit a nerve because someone attempted to poison you."

Tap, tap.

The sound of that *tap* was unmistakeably Snave. Fina opened the door a crack and waved him inside. She popped her head into the hallway, scanning left and right to be certain no one had followed him in.

"Ah, Snave." Lady Shillington banged her walking stick with approval.

Snave was doing his best to remain ever the good, impassive butler, but his widening eyes made this a difficult task. "I see m'lady's condition has improved."

"Take a seat, Snave." Fina pulled out a chair.

"Thank you, miss, but I prefer to stand, if it's not too much trouble." Snave surveyed the proffered chair as if Fina were asking him to sit on a wild boar.

"Fina, I'm rather thirsty – for an alcoholic drink. Do you have anything hidden away in your room?" Lady Shillington's eyes gleamed as she uttered the word 'drink'.

Fina scanned the room as if that would solve the problem. "No, I'm afraid not."

Snave leaned forward a quarter of an inch. "I will fetch you some brandy, m'lady."

Everyone yelled "no" in unison. Snave took two steps backward as if being pushed by a gale force wind.

Pixley rummaged around in his jacket pocket and removed a thin silver flask that resembled a cigarette case. "I keep this for these types of situations. Thirty-year-old single malt scotch."

Fina wrinkled her nose. "Scotch tastes like filthy socks."

"I'll ignore that remark, young Aubrey-Havelock," said Pixley with a grin. He swiped two glasses from a nearby table and poured a good measure into each. Pixley was so careful with the procedure, he looked like he was conducting one of Ruby's chemistry experiments.

"Snave, would you like to join us?"

"No. Thank you, Mr Hayford." Snave stiffened at the suggestion.

"Cheer up, Snave. See? I haven't been poisoned. Let's see you in the proper Christmas spirit." Lady Shillington offered Pixley another glass to fill.

In due course, Snave did as he was ordered. And though he remained in the same position, Fina detected a slight loosening of the facial muscles.

The sight of everyone enjoying their scotch made Fina's stomach rumble. She struggled from her plush seat and lumbered toward the tallboy in the corner, bringing out a box of chocolates.

"Aha!" Ruby smiled. "Now we can definitely salute your aunt's health."

Ruby rooted around in the box until she found her favourite square caramels.

Fina loved them all. She selected a round truffle and bit into the hard outer shell. "Mmh ... heaven."

Glancing up from her ecstasy, she saw her aunt, Pixley, and even Snave smiling at her. A flash of heat flowed across her face. To cover it, she approached each person with the box of chocolates.

Ruby wiped her fingers on her grandmother's blue handkerchief. "I have a proposition that will allow us to use Lady's Shillington's apparent poisoning to our advantage. I propose we lay a trap."

"For whom?" Pixley bit into a chocolate covered in nut shavings. "For the murderer or for the thief?"

"If everything turns out, it will be for both."

Ruby smoothed her hair. A sly smile was spreading across her face, as if she were a cat who had slurped up the cream.

"I'm ready for your plan, Miss Dove. I've heard more about your adventures with Fina and Pixley, and I'm impressed." Lady Shillington thumped her walking stick once more.

"That's very generous of you. But I must keep everyone somewhat in the dark. Except Snave, that is."

Fina stuck out her bottom lip. "But you never let us in on your secrets."

"Stop that whingeing, girl." The older version of Lady Shillington showed. Fina's lip resumed its normal position.

"I'll just step into my room with Snave, if you don't mind." Ruby ignored Fina's outburst.

As Ruby and Snave departed, Pixley swished his scotch around in his glass and stared into it, as if it would provide the answer to the meaning of life. He glanced up. "Lady Shillington, I have a question for you about your invitations." He paused. "I can see the connection of the guests to your brother's murder, but I'll admit I'm stumped when it comes to Cecily and Celestia Swift. What possible connection do they have?"

Lady Shillington smiled. "Yes, I imagine that must be puzzling to you. Besides having connections with Lord Strathclyde, Cecily was – well, how do you young people say it these days? She was courting your brother, Fina. Or perhaps it was the other way around."

Fina popped up from her seat, as jumpy as a flea. "That's it!" She stamped her foot. "I knew there was a reason they seemed so familiar. I remember seeing one of them with my brother in the village a few times. But she didn't live in the village, so I didn't think much of it. And Connor was very secretive about his relationships. It was the opposite of how he was in every other area of life."

Pixley studied Fina. "Do you think it has anything to do with what he mentioned in the letter to you?"

"What letter?" Lady Shillington's face went from puzzlement to injury in three seconds flat.

"Oh, ah, it was a letter Connor had written to me, before he ..." Fina hurried to find the letter in her nightstand in order to avoid bursting into tears.

But the letter had vanished.

"Selkies and kelpies." Fina uttered her favourite expression as if it were a statement of fact rather than an exclamation.

"Consider it this way – it means we're definitely on to something if that letter disappeared." Pixley took another sip of his scotch, completely unconcerned.

"Let us not be carried away by it," Lady Shillington said in a kind but firm voice. "Tell me what the important bits were in the letter."

Fina sighed and slumped down on the bed. "Something about what happens when you lick honey from a briar. And that we'll know those who don't love us by their limping."

"Your brother always had a flair for the dramatic. I'm not acquainted with anyone who has a limp, so I assume it wasn't meant in a literal sense. And as for honey, I suppose it's a reference to the honey shop." Lady Shillington set her mouth in a grim line. "I suppose it means that the murderer is among us, and that Connor was betrayed in some way. Which is certainly the case if he was framed for murder."

Ruby and Snave returned to the room. Snave's eyes glistened. Not from tears, but clearly from admiration.

"You two look pleased as punch." Pixley resumed his relaxed position on the sofa. "Tell us, oh great one, where your minions are supposed to go."

Ruby moved around to the back of the sofa and encircled her arms around his shoulders. "Dear Pix, where would I be without you as my little minion?" She giggled. "You're the best." She gave him a playful little slap on the shoulder.

"I know the feeling, Pixley." Fina grinned. "Sometimes I swear I'm piffy on a rock bun."

"Where do you children find these expressions?" Lady Shillington shook her head more in wonderment than exasperation.

Snave cleared his throat. "If I may, Lady Shillington, I believe etymologists trace the phrase to the music hall stage. Americans have a near-equivalent expression: 'bump on a log'."

"Thank you, Snave." Lady Shillington hid a smile behind her princess sleeve. "Where would we be without you?"

"I rather think you would be without a butler."

"Now. What is the plan of action?" Lady Shillington raised herself by her walking stick and then suddenly plopped back down from the effort. "Too much scotch at once," she giggled.

"I encourage you to sleep it off in Fina's bed." Ruby went over and turned back the bedspread.

"Not until I hear about this plan of yours."

"Ahem." Snave put a hand to his mouth. "The young lady assures me, Lady Shillington, it is better that you not know in advance what will happen. We will tell you all once we finish."

"Balderdash." Lady Shillington waved her cane about.

"Auntie, do cooperate. Trust me, I've had to have faith in Ruby without being able to fathom what could possibly come next. If she says it shall be so, it is better that way."

Lady Shillington ambled toward the bed, despite her crestfallen countenance.

Ruby touched Lady Shillington on the shoulder as she leaned against the bed. "I promise we'll tell you everything in due course. Just as soon as we catch the devils."

33

It was dark. Very dark.

"Oof." Fina bumped her knee against something hard. "Turn on the torch," she hissed.

A rattling sound ensued. "I can't get it to switch on," whispered Pixley.

"Here, I have a small one in my bag," whispered Ruby.

A small, weak spotlight appeared in front of Fina.

Then light flooded the room, revealing rows of chairs, a sofa, and an enormous screen in the back. A film projector stood near the front, partially hidden by a folding paper screen.

Fina glared at Snave. She leaned over to Ruby. "I thought he was supposed to leave the lights off."

"I do apologise." Snave bowed. "Since you extended the invitation, the earl and countess are most eager to enter the screening room. Shall I let them in now?"

"Yes, please do. No need for us to practise bumping around in the dark any longer." She held up her small torch. "At least we have one that works."

Snave said nothing, but nodded. He opened the door at the rear of the screening room. Felicity popped her head in, as if she were entering a forbidden, magical queendom. She frowned when she saw the trio standing near the last row of seats. They had dared to enter before her.

"What film are we screening?" She entered, followed by her husband and Noodle. "It is appropriate for children, I hope?"

Fina muttered under her breath, "Appropriate for children, yes. Appropriate for young monsters, no."

Pixley giggled. Noodle stuck out her tongue at them, but from behind her mother's skirts – well out of the line of sight of her parents.

"I've selected a Christmas tale. It has the rather unfortunate title of *Babes in Story Land*." Snave's vocal cords strained as he said the words.

"Good. Cecily said she wanted to see a jewel heist film and I said it would be most inappropriate for Beryl."

"Did you say my name?" Cecily and Celestia pushed past the Chivertons. "What a swell cinema," said Celestia.

Indeed, this new addition to Marsden Court was magnificent. Fina guessed that it must have been installed during the past year. She knew her aunt and uncle both enjoyed films, but she hadn't any idea they enjoyed them this much.

Uncle Harlan ambled in as if there wasn't anyone else present. He smiled at Fina, Pixley and Ruby as he passed and settled himself into a front-row seat.

Clive entered next. "Mmm... scrummy. Hope there are drinks coming with the film."

Penelope swept into the room, making what could only be described as a grand entrance. She wore a stunning light blue – almost white – chiffon gown. Or was it a robe? The way the light hit the chiffon made it glow like an apparition. "Am I late?" She held the up a hand to her forehead. Fina was sure she might bite her knuckle next.

"No, darling, you have impeccable timing." Bruno stamped

into the room, chomping at a cigar. "Get me a scotch," he snapped at Snave.

Pixley leaned over to Fina. "Someone is in a foul mood."

The Standishes loped in next, appearing rather worse for wear. Marjorie's hair was astray and Gerald looked like he had been sucking on a lemon. They said nothing as they made their way to their seats. Then Gerald turned on his heel.

"I say, are we going to have dinner tonight? I'm rather peckish. Tea only takes a chap so far. An army marches on its stomach."

"Cook is preparing an assortment of sandwiches that may be consumed in your seats." Snave shuddered. "Under the circumstances, and in consultation with Mr Fotheringham, we decided it would be disrespectful to sit down to dinner without Lady Shillington."

"And watching a film is less disrespectful?"

"According to Mr Fotheringham, yes, sir."

"Right, well, as long as I have the old feedbag, I don't care where we sit."

"Very good, sir."

Pixley took Fina aside as they moved toward their seats. "You don't think your aunt might be double-bluffing about the poisoning, do you?"

"Pixley!" Everyone's heads turned. "Sorry," said Fina sheepishly. Everyone turned back to their own little life concerns.

"No, I do not. How dare you make such an accusation." Fina somehow managed to whisper most vigorously.

"Sorry, Feens." Pixley was genuinely contrite. "I had to ask."

"Will you two stop chattering over there and come and join me?" Ruby gave them a steely smile.

As soon as everyone had settled into their seats, with sandwiches piled high on their plates and glasses full, Snave turned out the lights. The novel experience of watching a film in a house like this delighted Fina, especially when she could eat at the same time.

"Pssst." Ruby leaned over. "Don't get too comfortable. We need to leave soon."

A 'mmph' was all Fina could manage in reply.

The titles splashed across the screen as string music swelled. It was overdramatised, but Fina scolded herself for having ridiculously high standards. After all, here she was at Christmas, watching a lovely film with her friends, and, of course, eating a meal. But then she realised they'd have to leave soon – to spring whatever trap Ruby had cooked up this time.

"Time to leave. Everyone's in their seats." Ruby glanced at Fina and then at Pixley. They nodded and crept toward the door. Fortunately, the screen provided enough light that they didn't need a torch. Fina took exaggerated steps, praying her tendency to clumsiness wouldn't betray her.

Snave held the door open for them, just a crack. They snuck along like foxes about to raid a henhouse.

Still crouching over, and in single file, they made their way upstairs. Upstairs to Lady Shillington's room.

The only sound was an occasional burst of noise coming from the cinema, sporadically interspersed by a forceful gust of wind rattling the windowpanes.

Panther stood sentry in front of Lady Shillington's room, licking her paw. "Panther, what a good kitty," cooed Fina.

Ruby held a finger up to her lips. Fina nodded and stroked the cat. She had a sandwich in her pocket. Smoked salmon. She was glad to offer it to Panther as the odour bothered her.

There was no need to whisper, since all the guests were in the screening room and Lady Shillington was safely tucked away in Fina's bed. All the same, Ruby kept her voice as low as she could. "Fina and I will be behind the bed. Pixley, hide behind the door to the lavatory. When I give the signal, turn on the light switch."

Pixley and Fina nodded. Ruby unlocked the door and they crept in across the thick carpet. She turned on the weak torch.

Fina jumped, sinking her nails into Pixley's shoulder, and the pair of them let out a muffled cry.

There was someone lying in the bed.

34

It must be her aunt, playing a part.

Pixley opened the door to the lavatory and hid behind it. Ruby and Fina hid themselves behind the lumpy bed.

Fina hunched over in a little ball of nerves and tension. After about fifteen minutes, however, she relaxed. Whatever type of trap Ruby had set up probably wouldn't work. Too risky for the murderer or the thief. Unless ... perhaps the twins might use their devious drug concoction on everyone again? Those guests they'd seen in the winter garden had appeared woozy on their feet, but that was likely due to the steady diet of alcoholic beverages.

A branch scraped against the window. Perhaps it was a flying branch from the storm. The trees at Marsden Court stood well away from the sides of the house.

Ruby gripped Fina's hand. She listened.

There was a scraping noise and then a step. Scraping noise, and then a step. And it was definitely outside the door.

A small crack of light streamed in from the hallway. It grew larger and then disappeared as she heard the door give out a barely audible *click*.

Fina had a terrible urge to peer over the top of the bed. She had to see who it was. As she lifted herself on the heels of her feet, Ruby's hand on her shoulder stopped her. Pixley's eyes were shut as he stood behind the door. Was he asleep? Good Lord. So much for the dynamic trio.

The scraping noise began again, followed by a footstep.

Ruby took a small piece of paper out of her pocket, crumpled it up and hurled it at Pixley. It hit one of the glass panels on his spectacles. He jolted awake. His jolt caused the door to squeak a little on its hinges.

The sound must have been enough to spur whomever was in the room to action.

The bed moved.

A flash of silver.

Then the bed frame bounced as if someone were jumping on it.

Fina screamed. And screamed.

In horror, she realised someone was stabbing her aunt with a knife.

Pixley turned on the light, but it was too late. The attacker had already fled into the corridor.

Ruby and Pixley dashed into the hall. Fina stood by the bed, transfixed.

There was no blood. Only holes in the quilt. Little bits of down floated about the room as if it were snowing inside as well as outside.

She couldn't take it in. Throwing back the cover revealed a bolster and three pillows. A dummy! She certainly felt like one. Relief washed over her. And then it turned to anger. Why hadn't Ruby told her it wasn't her aunt in the bed?

And then she realised she was alone.

She hurried out of the room as if the pillows might rise up from the dead and attack her.

But a shiver of fear soon replaced the relief as she stood on the landing. Wherever Ruby and Pixley had chased the attacker to, it wasn't on this floor. And judging by the silence, they weren't even in the hall downstairs.

Sliding her hand down the cold banister rail, she descended with a cautious, almost regal step.

At the foot of the stairs, she tiptoed, even on the rug, in order to avoid making noise. She listened. But what was she listening for?

Shaking her head and deciding her slowness in reaching Pixley and Ruby was not helpful, she moved her feet rapidly.

As she passed the billiard room, she halted.

A scraping noise came from within. This scraping noise differed from the one the attacker had made. But it was a peculiar noise nonetheless. And it wasn't Panther's overgrown claws making that darling click-clack noise on the stone floor.

Fina stood frozen in front of the door, in a moment of indecision. Perhaps it would be better to fetch the others. But they were busy with more important things at the moment.

Her curiosity won out over her fear. She pushed the door open and eased her head around the corner.

A shadowy figure stood outside the French windows.

Fina made a gurgling noise that slowly crescendoed into another scream.

"Stop!" Pixley dashed after the hooded attacker, rounding one corner of the hallway a little too quickly. He slipped on a rug, toppling over onto his back.

He waved Ruby on as she bent down to help him up. "Keep going. We must find out who it is!"

For once, Ruby followed Pixley's orders. She kicked off her

heels and hurtled down the corridor and then down the stairs. The flapping, oversized gown with the hood moved toward the back stairs. Toward the cellar. Ruby dashed to the entrance.

Then she stopped. There was no way out of the cellar. She slammed the door shut and slid the barrel bolt into place.

Pixley appeared, limping and wincing.

"Where's the attacker? What happened?"

"He – or she – is in the cellar. There's no other exit, so I locked the door. I planned to follow, but then my survival instinct rose up."

"Good thinking. No need to be in a dark cellar with a killer."

"I'm not sure this person is a killer. At least, not a killer with intent."

Pixley's already-spectacle-magnified eyes widened. "What do you mean? This beast just brutally attacked those pillows, thinking they were Fina's aunt!"

Ruby leaned against the stone wall and sighed. "Yes, but this case has more twists and turns than any we've known. And no wonder, given the fact that the real murderer, or I ought to say the real perpetrator, got away with it for so long. But no longer."

"I'll fetch the others. At least we can figure out who it is by a process of elimination. And we can let the person in the cellar stew."

"Where's Fina?" Ruby straightened up. "I thought she was behind you."

Then they heard the scream. A scream like a cat who was about to attack another cat. A low, guttural growl that rises to a high pitch then ends in a hiss.

THE FIGURE RATTLED the handles of the French doors.

Fina took a tentative step closer.

"Fina! It's me, Ian," came the muffled cry.

"Ian!" The figure took shape, becoming a person she knew. Of course it was Ian. She could tell now by the way he was knocking on the windowpane.

After unlatching the door, Fina invited both Ian and the winter inside. The snow swirled in through the billiard room like an uninvited guest seeking a drink. The flakes flew at the fire before melting instantly in mid-air.

Ian did his best to shake off his own snow in a corner by the French windows. He looked like a snowman. His distinctive eyebrows were lined with frost and the top of his woollen hat had a dimple where a pile of snow had settled in.

Fina closed the door on the uninvited winter guest and helped Ian brush off the remainder of the snow.

"Fina! And – Ian!" Ruby cried from the doorway. "How did you ever make it through this blizzard?"

Ian's eyebrows wriggled as he gave her an amused, if rather self-satisfied smile. "Skis, dear Ruby, skis."

"But why take the risk of being carried away in a snowdrift?" Pixley glanced up from his task of warming his hands by the fire.

Ian's eyebrows lowered and his mouth set in a line. "After seeing you on the road to the village, I sensed something wasn't right. I knew that the three of you are such good sleuths the thief or murderer was bound to become a bit, shall we say itchy? That's why I knew I had to return."

He surveyed Ruby. Fina joined Pixley by the fireplace.

But Ruby wasn't in the mood. She said, "I am glad you're here and safe. We could use another brain right now to figure out what to do with the person in the cellar."

"Cellar?"

Ruby laid a hand on Ian's gloved hand and whispered in his ear.

He nodded and rolled one of the billiard balls down the table. It bounced off the side and rolled back.

"What are you two whispering about?" Pixley appeared as frustrated as Fina felt.

"Quickly, Ian! Do you hear those footsteps?" Ruby gave him a gentle shove. He took off in a trot toward the hallway, leaving a little trail of snow behind.

"M'lady?" Snave's head appeared, inch by inch, around the doorframe to the billiard room.

Alice's terror-stricken head appeared right below Snave's. "Miss, was that you screaming? It was awful! Are you injured, miss?"

Fina stepped forward. She knew what had to be done. "I screamed, Alice, though I am not injured." She paused. "Snave, please assemble everyone in the drawing room in fifteen minutes."

After Alice and Snave's heads disappeared, Pixley let out a low whistle as he rolled another billiard ball across the table. It disappeared into a corner pocket. "What a stroke of genius, Feens. Pre-empt the inevitable Miss Dove announcement."

One side of Ruby's mouth pulled back in scepticism. Then it relaxed into a smile. "You know me so well, Feens. Fowls that sleep in their roost are not hard to catch. That would be me, wouldn't it?"

Fina's stomach twitched as she realised what she had done. "It was out of turn, but I hope you can forgive me. After all, whoever is in the cellar can only stay there for so long."

"Quite right, quite right," Ruby sighed. "That's why I asked Ian to stand guard at the cellar door. I want to be sure the culprit doesn't escape."

Pixley chomped on his pipe. "It was Bruno Daniels, wasn't it?"

35

"Thank you, dear guests, for agreeing to assemble here. I'm certain we all wish to retire to bed, but there are a few things we must address before we can all rest easy in our beds tonight." Ruby laid her long arm across the mantel and surveyed the crowd. As she paused, all Fina heard was the slight crackling sound of snowflakes melting on the windowpane.

Pixley's deduction about Bruno Daniels had proven incorrect. At least regarding the mysterious attacker locked up in the cellar. Bruno sat on the edge of one of the sofas they had arranged in a semi-circle around the fire. He bent over as if he were going to be sick. Then his head flew backward as he leaned into the cushions.

Pixley himself sat rather awkwardly on a footrest next to Fina. All the other seats had been taken. Snave and Alice stood sentry at the door. In a wooden chair next to them sat Mrs Bramble, the cook. Though Mrs Bramble's heavy frame had a regal bearing to it, she appeared about as fidgety as a March wind. In contrast, young Noodle – hemmed in by both her parents – looked as warm and comfortable as an egg in a hen's behind.

She was the only one, however. And it was probably because she was staying up well past her bedtime.

As if on cue, Lady Chiverton said, "It's past time for me to tuck Beryl into bed. Please excuse me." She rose and held out a hand to Noodle.

"We've arranged for Mrs Bramble to attend to Beryl," coughed Snave. "I've had strict instructions from Mr Fotheringham that everyone – save Mrs Bramble and the child – should remain here in the drawing room."

Felicity eyed Uncle Harlan. Harlan's eyebrows lifted. Then his eyes widened as if he realised what role he was being asked to play. Lord of the Manor. He rubbed his hands in gleeful anticipation. "Most certainly, Snave," he said, his voice lowering an octave. "I'm afraid you'll need to stay, Lady Chiverton."

"Well, *really*," she said in a huff.

"I want to stay," whined Noodle.

Mrs Bramble looked enormously relieved to have an excuse to leave. Felicity bent down and whispered to Noodle. She began to cry. Crying wasn't the right word, however, for the irritating flatline sound, like a long screeching noise.

As the noise faded into the distance of the hall, audible sighs could be heard around the room. The previous tension-filled silence soon replaced the atmosphere of relief.

"Miss Dove, may we proceed? It is almost midnight," said Penelope, flopping her arm languidly on the back of the sofa behind Bruno's pained face.

"Yes, this farce has gone on long enough," intoned Basil. "I will not be subjected to this..."

Pixley held up a hand. "Please, Lord Chiverton." Basil glared at Pixley, but Pixley had eyes only for his pipe. "Ruby will explain everything."

"Thank you, Mr Hayford. As you all can see, one person –

besides Lady Shillington, who is recovering in her room – is missing." Ruby let the statement sink in.

"Yes, where has Gerald got to?" Cecily scanned the room. "I say, he's not been murdered, has he?"

A gasp came from Marjorie. Celestia put a calming hand on Cecily. "Is this true, Miss Dove?"

Ruby gave the twins a twisted smile. "What made you jump to the conclusion he was murdered, Miss Swift?"

Cecily held up a hand to her open red-rimmed mouth. "Oh, I just... after Lady Shillington..."

"Where is my husband, Miss Dove?" Marjorie's hair shone as she bent her head near the candle next to her. So close to the flame that Fina winced.

"Please, Mrs Standish. He is not injured. I'd like to address a few matters first before I explain his whereabouts. Depending on how you view the situation, we have three primary questions that need to be answered. First, who purloined Lady Chiverton's pearls and Lady Shillington's hatpins?"

"Hear, hear," interjected Lord Chiverton. Fina swore his combed-up eyebrows had grown an inch overnight.

"Second," continued Ruby, "who put hyoscine in Lady Shillington's tea – and why?"

"I thought it was an overdose of mistletoe tea that caused her to fall ill," said Clive. He stubbed an unlit cigarette against his case and then turned it over and repeated the motion.

Ruby shook her head. "No, that's what we were meant to think. I analysed the contents of her water glass, however, and found that it had been tainted with a drug called hyoscine. It produces similar effects to an overdose of mistletoe tea, but it's much stronger."

"Can't hyoscine kill you?" Celestia swung one crossed leg in a suspiciously vigorous manner.

Cecily nudged her sister in the ribs.

"How do you know that?" Pixley removed his pipe from his mouth as if he were Holmes asking the crucial question.

"I expect it's their interest in drugs," said Bruno, springing to life. "They were the ones who slipped the Benzedrine into our drinks, remember?"

Now it was Fina's turn to spring to life. "How did you figure out it was Benzedrine? I don't believe anyone knew that except us, Lord Chiverton, and Alice."

Bruno should have been renamed Beetroot Bruno at that moment. He stammered, "I – I – I'm sure one of them must have told me."

Cecily cooed, "It was me, remember, honey?"

Bruno gave her a sheepish smile but said nothing.

Ruby regarded the crowd as if they were a rather bothersome group of children. "And the third question is, who killed Fina's father?"

The only sound came from Alice rustling her apron.

The tension was thicker and stickier than the marmalade Fina enjoyed spreading all over her morning toast.

Everyone avoided looking at her.

Finally, Harlan spoke. "You're convinced it was someone other than Connor, Red?"

Fina nodded and pursed together her lips as tightly as she could.

Ruby cleared her throat. "Now that we've established the seriousness of this situation, let's begin at the beginning, with the pearls."

As Ruby had instructed her, Fina dangled the string of pearls she had found in the twins' room for everyone to see.

Felicity and Basil gasped.

"Don't tell me Miss Aubrey-Havelock is the thief," said Basil without a hint of sarcasm.

"No, Lord Chiverton. I found these pearls in the twins' room." Fina handed the pearls to Basil.

"Those are our pearls," said Celestia. "But they're ours, not the stolen ones."

"They're quite right," said Basil as he flung the pearls in disgust onto a nearby table. "Nothing but a string of pink paste. Fake."

"Think you're so smart, don't you?" Cecily sneered at Fina. "And what were you doing under our bed anyway? I don't buy that guff Mr Hayford fed us about you being drugged. We know the signs of that, don't we, Celestia?"

Bruno rolled his eyes.

"I was searching for the pearls. And I found them. Or what I thought were the stolen pearls." Fina decided to keep the bit about the anarchist literature to herself until Ruby chose to enquire about it.

Basil snorted and laid his hand over Felicity's. "Don't worry, my dear, we'll find your pearls soon."

Ruby took a sip of tea and replaced the teacup carefully in its saucer. "Would you like to tell your husband what really happened to those pearls, Lady Chiverton?"

36

Pixley cleared his throat. "It's better that you explain yourself, Lady Chiverton. You don't want to be tangled in this web of deceit and murder."

Felicity coughed. And then coughed again, uncontrollably.

Basil leapt up. "She's having an attack. Snave. We can carry her upstairs." He glared at Ruby. "Look at what you've done."

In a calm voice, Ruby replied, "Lady Chiverton. If you do not stop this charade now, you will regret it. We know all about how you sold your real pearls."

The coughing stopped. Felicity fell back into the cushions. She sighed and gazed at her husband. Then she pointed a finger at Alice. "It was she. She stole my pearls. I'm sure she's a member of the Forty Elephants Gang. They pose as maids, don't they?"

Penelope held up a finger. "And she wore that splendid gold lamé gown the night of the party. Where on earth would she have the funds for something like that?"

Alice gasped, and her thin veneer or professional servitude slipped yet again. "I never! What gang? I never stole them pearls. It's all lies!" She wiped her face with a corner of her apron. Fina thought back to Mrs Trumper's accusation that Alice had stolen hot cross buns from Mrs Bunney's teashop. Of course, it was Mrs Trumper, so anything was possible.

"You really are shameless, aren't you?" Ruby lost her even temper for a moment. "You'd have Alice go to jail for your own greed, Lady Chiverton?"

Penelope said, "But I have a point about the gown, don't I, Miss Dove?" She resembled a hopeful puppy.

"You do have a point. But it points back at Lady Chiverton, not Alice Ditton."

Felicity clenched her teacup and sighed. "It's true. The gown was mine, and—"

"She sold it to me!" Alice broke in, unable to keep quiet. "I had a few shillings put away, for Christmas, like, and when Lady Chiverton said she didn't need the frock, I said I'd take it for the price she wanted. It's such a grand frock, and I get so tired of wearing this drab stuff all the time." She twitched her mono-chrome skirt.

"She's right," said Felicity. "I needed the money, and I couldn't take the risk that my husband might find the dress and realise I'd bought it in a moment of madness. I love fashion, but he disapproves of all that. He thinks it's frivolous. And he gives me so little for an allowance. That's why I had to sell my pearls and replace them with artificial ones."

Defiant circles of red appeared on Felicity's otherwise pasty white face. Her voice rose as she stared at Basil. "You never give me anything. Our whole lives are just scrimp and save. All for that blasted boys' school full of little spoiled brats!"

Ruby held up a hand. "We appreciate that this family matter may need attending to, but now is not the time. You stole your own pearls. The fake ones, correct?"

But Ruby wasn't looking at Felicity anymore. She was staring at Basil. Felicity's eyes narrowed on her husband's shrivelled-apple face.

"You?!"

Basil shrank into his suit like a frightened turtle. "I, ah, well. I owe you an explanation, dear."

"Why don't you start with Carrot?" Ruby's eyes glimmered. She was having fun at Basil's expense. *Good show, Ruby Dove.*

"Carrot?" said everyone in unison.

Fina drifted back to that scene in the corridor with Noodle. Where she was talking about her stuffed rabbit. Stuffed. Large belly and cottontail.

"You stole your wife's pearls – not knowing they were fake – and then put them inside Noodle's stuffed rabbit named Carrot, didn't you?" Fina glowed.

Basil's mouth hung open in a most unbecoming manner. "But how? Where? When?" He stopped. "Yes, I, ah, took my wife's pearls and hid them in the stuffed rabbit." Then, in a rapid-fire voice, he said, "The school coffers were empty. Again. I needed money quickly. I thought..."

Pixley's journalist eyes lit up. "That you'd engage in a bit of insurance fraud?"

"It wasn't fraud, exactly. It was creative accounting."

"Well, well." Marjorie stretched her body like a cat and smiled. "Mr Morality engages in creative accounting? I wasn't aware schoolmasters could be so creative. I thought imagination was frivolous."

As Basil sputtered, Pixley intervened. "So you lifted the hatpins, too?"

Basil's jaw flapped open. "Hatpins? What the blazes are you on about?"

"We'll come to the hatpins in a moment, young man," said a voice from the doorway.

"Millie!" Harlan leapt up and embraced his sister-in-law. He stepped back and stared at her. "What are you doing out of bed? Shouldn't you be resting?"

Fina's aunt flung her newly acquired cane about with relish. "That's where someone in this room would like me to be, wouldn't they, Miss Dove?"

Penelope patted her friend on the shoulder and guided her to a chair near her own.

Ruby nodded. "And we must begin with Mrs Pritchard to answer that question."

Penelope pursed her lips. "Because I'm a herbalist?"

Pixley pointed his pipe at Penelope. "You were the one to prescribe her the mistletoe tea, weren't you?"

"Yes, but that would make me the least likely to poison her with it," sighed Penelope. She was clearly unmoved by these accusations. "And Miss Dove knows that perfectly well."

Ruby smiled. "It's true. And I cannot see a motive for you to kill your friend. Unless..."

"Unless my aunt saw something Mrs Pritchard wanted her to forget. Since that's one effect of hyoscine – forgetting."

"But why would someone want Lady Shillington to forget what she had seen?" Bruno leaned forward, genuinely interested.

"Because I invited you all here to find out who killed my brother and nephew. And while I only have a guess, I'm certain Miss Dove will reveal all."

37

Mumbling and grumbling erupted at this revelation. "I wasn't there," and "I didn't have anything to do with it," echoed around the room.

"Stop!" yelled Fina. She wagged a shaking finger around the room. "You'd better tell the truth now. Or else I'll – I'll..."

Pixley put a hand on Fina's elbow. "Fina is correct," he said in his best baritone. "Pearls and hatpins and temporary illness are all fun and games. This is serious. This is murder."

Until this moment, Ruby had held off pacing in front of the fire. At the introduction of the word 'murder' she began her habitual perambulation. Looking down at her well-shod feet, she said, "Let's continue with Mrs Pritchard, shall we?"

Penelope wriggled her toes inside her soft-covered slippers. The rest of her body remained motionless. Her eyelids, a beautiful silvery-blue, blinked rapidly. "I have no connection whatsoever with those tragic circumstances." She paused. "Though my dearly departed husband had business dealings with Hugh Aubrey-Havelock."

"What happened to your husband's money when the business went belly-up?" Pixley leaned forward.

"I was destitute," said Penelope. "One day, I came across an old herbalist book that had belonged to my grandmother. I became fascinated by it and began to prescribe remedies here and there for friends. Soon, they were consulting me."

"And then you thought you'd go straight for the money," sighed Lady Shillington. "And scrape a friendship with me based on your connection to my family." She stamped her cane. "But you are good at what you do, by golly, and I appreciate your company." Penelope smiled back at her friend.

"May we please get on with it? I'd really like to find out what happened to my husband." Marjorie drummed her perfectly manicured nails on the sofa.

"Quite so, Mrs Standish. I'll volunteer myself next." Harlan lifted a finger as if he were a schoolboy, eager to supply an answer.

"Yes, Mr Fotheringham," replied Ruby, just as a school-teacher would.

"Though I have a rather, well, *eccentric* exterior, old Harlan knows what's what," he said, tapping the side of his nose and winking at the crowd. "First, I had a motive to kill Hugh, I suppose, since he was a lovely person and a good businessman, at least in terms of running a small shop, though a terrible beekeeper. I loaned him money, and then more money, until it all became a rather drastic situation. You see, I needed the money to fund some of my experiments—"

"Like your radio hat?" laughed Clive.

Fina glared at him. "Be quiet, Clive."

"You mean your replication of polyethylene?" Ruby grinned.

"You heard about it, too? I thought it was only the twins who knew," said Harlan. He held up a warning finger. "Someone had been snooping in my workshop. I keep the chemical formula for polyethylene there in a safe. Fortunately, the twins couldn't open it."

Cecily and Celestia squirmed in their seats.

"How did you figure out it was the twins searching your workshop?" Clive gawped at his uncle.

"Because I found a few strands of red hair. The only people with red hair this weekend are the twins, and, to a lesser degree, old Red here." He winked at Fina.

Cecily snorted. "A few strands of hair? Please. You must do better than that."

Harlan pounded his fist on an end table. "My workshop is immaculate. I trust no one. I check and recheck everything. Even though I trust Millie with my life, I wasn't so certain about the crowd she invited to Marsden Court for the weekend."

"Why would anyone want to steal your formula?" Fina asked.

"I imagine it could be a powerful addition to military equipment," Ruby said. "My chemistry tutor told me about it."

Nodding dejectedly, Harlan said, "Precisely. I have no intention of it falling into the hands of anyone connected to the military – anywhere. But it could fetch a pretty price if someone stole the formula."

Fina coughed. "Such as those connected to various political organisations? Anarchists or communists, for example?" She levelled her gaze at the twins.

Bruno pointed his cigar at the twins. "Yes. I remember seeing bolshie literature in their bedroom. What, were you planning on selling the formula to the Germans? The Russians? The Italians? Or an autonomous organisation?" He twisted the cigar around in his fingers. "I knew there was something peculiar about you two."

The twins crossed their arms together and gazed at one another. Cecily said, "You know very well why we had that literature, *Lord Strathclyde*. You told us to create a diversion that, if we were discovered, would cover our real employers."

"What rot. Codswallop." He waved his cigar airily.

Celestia turned to Ruby. "What does all of this have to do with the murder of Hugh Aubrey-Havelock?"

"A great deal. Your sister was seen stepping out with Connor Aubrey-Havelock. And we have a photo to prove that she knew a few of you sitting around this circle."

Cecily pouted. "It's true I was seeing Connor for a while, but that hardly has anything to do with the murder."

"But if you're Bolshies then it might well have something to do with it," said Bruno.

"How?" inquired Pixley. "Just because they're anarchists they would kill the father of one of the young men Cecily was seen with?"

Fina closed her eyes. She remembered the bit of newsprint that said Bruno was not what he seemed. Could it have anything to do with the fact he was trying to implicate the twins?

As if in answer to Fina's thoughts, Celestia said, "Admit it, Bruno. It was you who hired us. You were the one who asked us to steal the formula."

38

"You're off your chump," Bruno said, unconcerned by the accusations. "Would you like to prove what you're saying?" Fina detected a definite threatening note below the breezy exterior.

Cecily squeaked, "You hired us to steal the formula. You work for the British government."

"I do, dear girl, I work for the British government. A member of parliament obviously works for the government." He waved his cigar at the crowd. "The ravings of drug-addled brains, ladies and gentlemen. I ask you."

Fina nodded at Ruby and withdrew the scrap of newsprint from her pocket.

Mrs Bramble slipped back into the room. The little blighter must have fallen asleep.

"Ah, Mrs Bramble, thank you for rejoining us," said Ruby.

Holding the slip of paper aloft, Fina said, "Someone left this scrap of paper in my bag. It says that Bruno Daniels isn't who he says he is."

Before Fina knew what was happening, Bruno grabbed the note from her and threw it into the fire.

"My, my, *Lord Strathclyde*," said Pixley with a touch of glee. "Why are you so upset by a scrap of paper?"

Fina saw Ruby give Mrs Bramble an almost imperceptible nod.

"Ahem," said Mrs Bramble. All heads turned. "It was me."

Ruby said, "You wrote it on a piece of paper torn from a cookbook, didn't you, Mrs Bramble?"

Mrs Bramble's eyes widened and she clasped her hands together. "Yes, miss. I overhead a conversation between him and Hugh Aubrey-Havelock over a year ago. That was when the two were visiting Marsden Court." She turned to Fina. "My dear Miss Aubrey-Havelock, there's something you must know. Your father worked for the British government. He was a spy."

Gasps.

The room spun. Pixley put an arm around Fina, steadying her.

"A spy for the British government?" asked Pixley.

Mrs Bramble nodded. "That's right, sir. Bruno Daniels is, too. Or at least he was at the time. I overheard them talking about their orders from SIS. That's the intelligence services, I believe? They thought the kitchen was a safe place to chat, especially if the cook was absent. I didn't think much of it until later. It began to make sense why your father was always meeting people at Marsden Court."

"Why didn't you say anything at the time?" Pixley followed up.

"It wasn't my place, was it? Besides, what would it have to do with young Connor killing his father?"

"But why leave a note for Fina about it now?"

Mrs Bramble pushed back a wisp of hair that had fallen forward from her bun. "I dunno. I felt bad that I hadn't told Miss Aubrey-Havelock. And then Alice, here, told me about everything that was going on upstairs. The pearls, then Lady Shilling-ton, and I thought, well, my mind would rest easier if I told her to at least keep an eye on Lord Strathclyde."

"It doesn't make any sense," said Fina. "Why would my father work for the British government?"

Bruno sighed. "Even if I were to deny it, you'd all still think it's true."

As she rubbed her temples, Fina said, "But my father would never work for the intelligence services. My mother would never have allowed it."

"Maybe he kept it a secret from her," said Clive.

She shook her head again. "No, I cannot accept it. There must be another explanation."

Ruby looked at Mrs Bramble. "Do you remember anything about the content of their conversation?"

Fina stared at Bruno as Mrs Bramble hemmed and hawed. The cigar he clenched between his teeth threatened to split in half and fall to the floor. He shut his eyes, as if he were praying.

"Funny," said Mrs Bramble. "Now that you mention it, there was something. I remembered it at the time because it was like my last name – bramble. What was it now… thorn, no. Nettle, no."

"Was it *briar*, Mrs Bramble?" asked Ruby. The corner of her mouth lifted. Fina knew this meant she had solved the case.

Mrs Bramble jumped halfway out of her seat. "That's it! Briar! I don't remember anything else. Only briar. The conversa-tion started off friendly enough, but Lord Strathclyde became as bad-tempered as a weasel, he did."

Bruno said nothing.

Lady Shillington rose to her feet, though she still leaned on her cane. Her mouth and shoulders drooped. "I swore to your father, Red, that I'd never tell a soul. But if we are ever to get to the bottom of this case, I think I'd better tell you. Especially because the word 'briar' seems to mean something to Miss Dove here."

"Please, Lady Shillington, I'd be most grateful," said Ruby. She sat on the edge of a sofa so Lady Shillington could take centre stage in front of the fireplace.

"As some of you know, I invited you all down here this weekend because of your connections – however tenuous – with the murder of my brother and nephew. I say murder of my nephew because whoever killed Hugh just as surely killed Connor."

Tears streamed down Fina's face but she did nothing to stop them. Pixley passed her a handkerchief.

"Dear Red," said Lady Shillington, staring into Fina's eyes, "you're absolutely correct that your father wouldn't work for British intelligence."

Bruno perked up. "What do you mean? Of course he did."

"He was *employed* by British intelligence," said Lady Shillington, "but he *worked* for the Irish home rule movement for the past twenty years. That's how he met your mother, Red. Even though they told the story a bit differently."

Fina's mouth dropped open. "But they said they met when they lived in London – through a friend of a friend. You mean that wasn't true?"

Lady Shillington sighed. "It was only a lie by omission. It is true that they met in London. They also met through a friend of a friend. A friend who happened to also be in the resistance. Your mother and father agreed I had to play a part – to act as if your mother marrying into the family was unsatisfactory. I went along with their wishes, even though it was against my better judgment."

Bruno made a gurgling, strangled noise. He couldn't speak, but Fina couldn't care less about his emotional state.

Ruby leaned in to deliver the final blow. "That's why," she said, "you killed him, Lord Strathclyde."

39

Thwack.

Lady Shillington's cane came down on Bruno's shoulder. Again. Ruby and Clive restrained her. "You devil! You killed Hugh and Connor!"

Ruby whispered in her ear as she helped her into a nearby chair. Whatever magic words Ruby uttered had the effect of calming Lady Shillington. Her eyes still bored into Bruno's, however.

"I did no such thing, Miss Dove, and you are perfectly aware of it."

"Then tell us about your conversation with Hugh Aubrey-Havelock about *briar*."

"Damn you," he growled.

"Enough of that, you pompous twit," said Clive. He grinned as if he had been wanting to say that phrase his whole life.

"'Briar' was the name of an agent," sighed Bruno. "I wanted to assign this agent to a case, and Hugh strongly disagreed with it. But that was hardly enough to make me murder the blasted fellow! And yes, before you ask, the twins are here to find the formula on my behalf, which is on behalf of the intelligence services. We need that formula before anyone else gets their hands on it. I thought our little scheme about the film plans would be enough to have us all invited together."

"But why the twins, Lord Strathclyde? Surely, in your professional position, you have access to plenty of more experienced agents who can do your dirty work for you?" asked Ruby.

He smirked. "That's as may be but I assure you, Cecily and Celestia have excellent form in this area."

Pixley could hold back no longer. "The gang! That's it, isn't it? They're in the Forty Elephants!"

Gasps. Fina shot Pixley an admiring glance, but everyone else was gaping at the twins.

Celestia rolled her eyes. "That's torn it!"

"Good work, Pix," said Ruby, smiling. "Poor Alice was blamed for the thefts, but in fact it was the Swifts who had light fingers. Running with a fast crowd in London like they do, they need money – lots of it – and there's no shortage of dodgy types among their circle of friends. Bruno knew what was going on, and exploited their talents accordingly. No doubt he made them an offer they couldn't refuse."

"Astonishing. Didn't you say earlier they were Bolshies?" Gerald piped up.

"That was all a cover. No self-respecting socialist would let a servant take the rap for her own criminal acts," said Ruby.

From across the room, Alice gave her a grateful nod.

As one unit, the twins stood up and began edging toward the door. "We're just stepping out for the tiniest second..." one began. But a loud *crack* brought them to a halt.

Marjorie put a hand on Bruno's arm. "What's that noise? It's coming from the hallway."

"It sounds like splitting wood," said Penelope.

"He's getting away!" came Ian's voice from the hallway.

Everyone dashed into the hallway, save Lady Shillington.

They ran toward the cellar. Ian had thrown his body against the door, though he was clearly fighting a losing battle as a foot – presumably belonging to Gerald – was wedging the door partially open.

"Let me out! Let me out!" yelled Gerald.

"Ian, do as he says." Ruby squeezed Ian's hand.

Ian slid back the bolt and out stepped a dishevelled Gerald. The hooded cloak was covered in dirt and dust and what little remained of his hair was standing on end.

"Well?" He scanned the faces of the assembled crowd. "Why did you lock me in the cellar?"

"Perhaps a better question, Mr Standish, is why are you wearing a hooded cloak?" Penelope asked with a wry smile.

"And why did you try to murder my aunt?" asked Fina, shivering. She asked the question with childlike curiosity.

Pixley removed his jacket and put it over Fina. "Ruby, may we go back to the drawing room? No sense in shivering out here. I think Fina is in shock."

"I most certainly am," she mumbled as he piloted her back to the drawing room.

Snave, ever the thoughtful butler, had already prepared a tray of brandy for everyone in the drawing room. The room had a festive atmosphere, although the return of the shocked, scared and perplexed group of people shifted the mood.

Fina downed her snifter in one gulp.

"Good for you, Feens," said Pixley, finding a rug to put on Fina's knees.

Her teeth began to chatter. Pixley gave her another glass of brandy. That was better.

"Now, tell us what this is all about, Mr Standish," said Ruby.

"Where's Marjorie?" asked Basil.

Ruby padded into the hallway.

"I expect she went to powder her nose," said Felicity.

Gerald looked dubious but removed his cloak. "Very well. I'm not proud to admit this, but there's nothing for it now. I tried to kill you, Lady Shillington. I thought you knew something about Hugh's death."

"Why would you kill me if I knew something about Hugh's death? Are you telling us that you murdered Hugh?"

Gerald coughed. "Yes. I did. I overheard you talking to Harlan about Hugh's death. About how he was an agent."

"Forgive me, Mr Standish, but what does that have to do with Hugh's death and, more particularly, you?" Lady Shillington asked.

"Where's Ruby?" asked Fina, glancing up from her brandy-induced stupor.

Ruby returned from the hallway. Her hair was askew, as was her skirt.

"Marjorie has vanished."

A SEARCH PARTY set out around the house. Ian, Ruby and Pixley arranged it. Fina blinked her eyes and stayed huddled on the sofa. Occasional whoops and hollers floated in from the hallway.

After staring at the floodlight on the falling snow outside for at least thirty minutes, Fina tilted her head back into the cushions. Little snowflake dots appeared in her vision when she closed her eyes. She began to drift. The fire was warm, and her consumption of brandy helped her to fall asleep.

Something slithered. In her dreamlike state, she imagined it was Noodle's snake.

Jerking her head upward, she tried to open her eyes, but they fell closed again straight away.

A gloved hand wrapped around her throat. Another slid across her mouth.

"If you do anything, I'll break your neck, you understand?" The voice sounded muffled, as if the speaker were wearing a scarf.

Fina blinked her assent.

"I have a good mind to kill you right now. But I'd rather you lived in torment."

Why torment? Hadn't she been tormented enough? Fina strained through her brandy-addled brain to place the voice.

Marjorie.

With this realisation she struggled and flailed about, even though she knew it wasn't a clever idea.

"Didn't you hear me, you brat?" Marjorie hissed. "Stay still. I want you to understand what happened so you can replay it over in your mind, again and again for the rest of your life."

Fina gave up the struggle.

"Your father was a snivelling, two-timing, two-bit operative. He was going to tell Bruno that I worked for the Germans. That's why he had to go. He thought I had some allegiance to that nutcase they call Hitler. Were you aware that Schicklgruber is his real name? At least that's what British journalists say," she laughed. "The joke was on your father, though, because I work for whoever I want. Still, I couldn't let him ruin my livelihood. After I hit Hugh on the head that day in the shop, Connor saw me leaving. At four o'clock. He was the only one to see me leave. I began to cry uncontrollably and play the damsel in distress. After saying his father had been murdered and that I had discovered the body, I told him they'd convict me. He fell for it. Then I seduced him. And let him go to the gallows."

"Mmmmph," said Fina.

"Ah, you want to know why I let him be executed? Your brother was always one for word games. He also had a photographic memory. I was certain he had seen notes from a 'Briar' somewhere in the shop. It was only a matter of time before he figured out what had really happened. I couldn't take that chance, so I was one of the anonymous witnesses for the police. Besides, the longer the crime remained unsolved, the more likely it would be the police would find something. And not just something about the murder, but something about my activities as an agent. I couldn't take that chance."

Fina made a gurgling noise again, hoping it would keep Marjorie talking. Surely someone would come to look in on her soon?

The cool silk of a scarf floated across Fina's neck. Then it tightened.

Marjorie hissed in her ear, "I could kill you right now." The scarf shifted to Fina's mouth. "But I'll do the next best thing. I'll gag you while I make my escape. Tell your friends not to try anything. I'm armed. And I will shoot."

Fina had always wondered why it had been called a gag. And now she knew. As Marjorie tightened it around her mouth, bitter bile crept up her throat. Fortunately, it loosened a smidgen when she had finished tying the knot. Though Marjorie had somehow tied it to the sofa so she couldn't lift her neck at all.

"I have a message I'd like you to deliver," Marjorie cackled. "Tell Miss Ruby Dove that I have a bone to pick with her. We'll be in touch, I'm certain of that."

40

"Fina!" yelled Ian.

He jumped over a chair and a table as if he were running a steeplechase. Soon, her mouth was free and she could sit up.

"Marjorie was here," she gasped. "She must have escaped. Have you searched outside?"

"Snave and Clive have been standing guard over all the cars outside, so she can't have escaped that way."

Pixley and Ruby burst in. "Are you hurt, Fina?"

She shook her head. "Just a little sore. I'm shaking again, though this time it's from anger."

"I don't understand it," said Pixley. "We've searched everywhere. And she'd be a fool to walk away in this snow."

"Skis!" Fina jumped up. "Ian's skis!"

Ruby glared at Ian.

Ian held up his hands. "That was the first thing I checked when we began to search. The skis were where I had left them."

Ruby's crossed arms relaxed. She shrugged.

Pixley snapped his fingers. "I've got it! I remember reading about priest holes, as a child. Marsden Court is old enough to have one, isn't it?"

Fina tapped her teeth. Ruby smiled at her mimicking gesture. "I remember once that Snave let us into a priest hole when we were children. But I thought he said it was blocked off."

"Let's find out."

Fina dashed to the library with Ian, Ruby and Pixley in tow. Once inside the chilly room, Fina stood with her hands on her hips and closed her eyes. "If I could only recall..." she said to herself.

She ran a finger across the books. First one shelf, then another. "Aha!" she said when she came to *Hard Times* by Dickens. A whir and a creak came from behind the wall as she pulled out the book. Then a bookcase popped open.

Pixley clapped his hands with childish glee. Ian and Ruby glared at him but smiled when they saw he already had a torch with him. He switched it on and waved it inside. Ian was the first to stick his neck into the gloom. Turning around, he said, "Someone has been in here recently. The cobwebs are torn in a pattern. And I can see little dusty footprints on the floor. They look like heels."

"That tears it, then," said Ruby. "She must have escaped that way."

"Well, what are we waiting for?" asked Pixley. "Let's go after her!"

Fina grabbed Pixley's shoulder. "Wait. She's probably already made it all the way through the tunnel. It's night-time. And she might have a car at the other end. I think she planned her escape in advance. The most important point, however, is that she is armed."

Ian said, "Fina's right. I'm trained for this situation and I don't think we should go after her. I'm familiar with her sort and I'm sure she planned it in advance. It would be dangerous."

Vindicated by Ian, Fina nodded. "Marjorie also told me to

tell Ruby that she would be seeing her again. And that she had a bone to pick with her."

"That settles it," said Ian. "We're not going anywhere. No need to put Ruby in danger."

Ruby's contorted face expressed her internal battle over Ian's protectionism and her independence. Her exhaustion won out in the end, however.

Snave materialised out of the ether. He had an envelope on a silver salver.

"Lady Shillington requests your presence in the drawing room." He handed Fina the envelope. It was postmarked London, but had no return address. She'd read it later.

"Would you tell her that I'll tell her all in an hour or two?" Fina asked with pleading eyes. "Tell her that everything is resolved and that she should take a nap."

"Very good, miss."

"Would you all mind very much if we retired to my bedroom?"

"Feens!" said Pixley, scandalised.

"Leave her be, Pix," said Ruby.

Fina gave them all a wan smile. "I'll lie down in bed and then we can finally put this all to rest. At least for the moment."

IAN, Pixley and Ruby sat in various states of repose around Fina's green room. Pixley stretched out on a settee, while Ruby and Ian sat together in two chairs, side by side.

"That is quite a story," said Ruby. "I wonder what Marjorie has in store for us. Or for me."

"I'm sure we'll find out soon enough," sighed Fina. "But I'm relieved to finally understand what happened. She must have been the one to put nails in our tyres. And she must have stolen Connor's letter. Did you know it was Marjorie all along, Ruby?"

"It's irritating to say yes, but may I say yes? I knew there had to be more to the story, as you suspected. Since you told me Connor was fond of word games, I thought about the words in his letter. It wasn't long before I figured out that Marjorie's maiden name, Riber – the one we saw on the back of the photograph – was an anagram for *Brier*. It's spelled slightly differently, of course, but it was the only link that made any sense. Then I needed to goad Bruno into spilling the beans, as they say. Then it all came together."

Fina sighed. "Here I was, seeking someone with a limp. I was completely on the wrong track!"

"Connor put in his fair share of red herrings, though this could have referred, I suppose, to Marjorie being not what she seemed," said Ruby. "But there was real emotion in that letter. He meant it when he said he hoped God would hold you in the palm of his hand."

Fina managed a watery smile through incipient tears.

"Why did Gerald say it was him? Was he protecting Marjorie?" asked Pixley.

"Poor sap. He was so in love with Marjorie, he would do anything. Even though he's not the sharpest knife in the drawer, I suspect he figured out she was somehow involved in what was going on. Perhaps he found the stolen hatpins."

"Why did Marjorie steal the hatpins?" asked Fina.

"She saw an opportunity to use the pearl theft to her advantage. Because she suspected Lady Shillington knew something or had seen something this weekend, she wanted her to forget. Perhaps she wanted to kill her. Either way, the hatpin theft was a convenient ruse to throw us off the scent. It would look like a thief had incapacitated Lady Shillington in order to steal the hatpins after stealing the pearls."

"How does Bruno fit into all of this?" asked Pixley.

"He probably assumed the twins stole the hatpins. And with their record, they could hardly prove they hadn't. I don't believe Bruno has any notion how dangerous Marjorie really is. She had him well and truly hoodwinked. To him, she was just a pretty face with a talent for telling porky-pies." Ruby sighed. "The arrogance of our elected representatives never fails to astound me."

They sat in silence for a moment.

"There's one more loose end," said Fina. "Basil's aftershave. Why was he wearing my father's aftershave?"

"Felicity was in love with your father. We discussed the possibility before," said Ruby. "There's no reason to believe he reciprocated. But she visited the shop the day he died. I believe she bought her husband the aftershave as a reminder."

"That's a little, well, peculiar, isn't it?" Ian scratched his head.

"Felicity is a little peculiar, though," said Fina. "And I'd probably do odd things if I were married to Count Dracula. No doubt that's why she spent all her money on that outrageous dress: hoping to impress her beloved Hugh. And once he was gone, there was no need for her to keep it. It probably took her some time to reach that conclusion, but when she did she sold it to Alice."

"Thank goodness we managed to clear Alice's name, as well as your brother's, Feens," said Ruby.

Ian laid a hand over Ruby's. "I'm worried about you, Ruby ... and Fina. Even if the police are now off your back, there's still this Marjorie character, and she's infamous in my circles."

Ruby looked aghast. "Then why didn't you tell us about her?"

"No, no," he said. "I misspoke. What I meant was that 'Briar' is legendary. 'Triple agent' doesn't even begin to describe it. He – or, as I now know, she – is an agent for hire. And extremely dangerous. I think it would be a good idea for you to leave England for a while. Even if it's only for a short while."

Fina sighed. "Perhaps. She certainly terrified me." She hit her hand down on the bed. It met the envelope Snave had brought for her earlier.

She tore it open.

"Read it, Fina!" called Pixley.

Her face turned warm. Then it turned hot as she read the letter.

"I'll play Sherlock for once," said Pixley. "It's from Idris, isn't it, Red?"

Fina nodded.

Pixley glanced at the mistletoe in the corner and winked at Ian and Ruby.

"Idris says he wants to meet in Lisbon. For the New Year."

The End

Continue Ruby and Fina's adventures with *The Mystery of Ruby's Roulette!*

If you enjoyed *Ruby's Mistletoe*, I'd be grateful for a brief review or simple rating (Australia, Germany, UK, or US). Reviews help readers discover this book. Thank you, dear reader!

Join my readers' group for updates and goodies!

FORTY ELEPHANTS GANG?

The Forty Elephants Gang lasted from the 1870s through the 1950s.

Check out this article from *The Guardian* if you want to know more. Enjoy!

MORE MYSTERIES

The Ruby Dove Mystery Series follows the early adventures of our intrepid amateur-spy sleuths:

With many cases under their fashionable belts, Ruby and Fina are ready for more in *Partners in Spying Mysteries:*

ABOUT THE AUTHOR

Rose Donovan is a lifelong devotee of golden age mysteries. She now travels the world seeking cosy spots to write, new adventures to inspire devious plot twists, and adorable animals to petsit.

www.rosedonovan.com
rose@rosedonovan.com
Reader Group
Follow me on Bookbub
Follow me on Goodreads

NOTE ABOUT UK STYLE

Readers fluent in US English may believe words such as "fuelled", "signalled", "hiccough", "fulfil", "titbit", "oesophagus", "blinkers", and "practise" are typographical errors in this text. Rest assured this is simply British spelling. There are also spacing and punctuation formatting differences, including periods after quotation marks in certain circumstances.

If you find any errors, I always appreciate an email so I can correct them! Please email me at rose@rosedonovan.com. Thank you!

For Baba

Made in the USA
Middletown, DE
18 November 2023

43034450R00130